Twenty Terrifying Tales From Our

TECHNO FEUDAL TOMORROW

WILLIAM KHERBEK

Arcadia Missa Publications
35 Duke Street
London
W1U 1LH

www.arcadiamissa.com
@ArcadiaMissa
info@arcadiamissa.com

TWENTY TERRIFYING TALES FROM OUR TECHNOFEUDAL TOMORROW, 2021

Cover artwork by

ISBN: 978-1-8382840-1-5

Arcadia Missa Publications are available from the gallery, our website and selected stockists.

Politicraft in the Age of the Firm

In previous eras, the lives of people were placed at the mercy of arbitrary accidents of history. The social organisation that dominated the world for the centuries preceding the rationalisation was known as a 'state', often designated as a 'nation-state'- a particularly repugnant variant of the concept, if a historian may be allowed an opinion - in which an essentially arbitrarily defined group of people living in a territory were believed, somehow, to have greater legitimacy within an emergent state by virtue of some occult property or other of their ethnic or cultural lineage. Entire intellectual systems were designed to indemnify this misbegotten proposition. Students of the early period of politicraft will be familiar with oxymoronic notions like 'race science' and pseudosciences like phrenology which were an integral part of this project, as was, to the chagrin of many literature students of today, entire bodies of so-called 'national literatures', a term that is absurd to contemporary life, but one must rest grimly assured, expressed the fervent hopes, dreams, and visions of entire populations. The risibility of such ideas belies their danger.

At the time of writing, we are nearly a century on from the foreclosure of the last territory that defined itself according to the properties and appurtenances of the old 'nation state' system. In point of fact, the great survivor of these grand ideas and ideological edifices was a curious principality in Southern Africa known as Eswatini. In its foreclosure, wherein its supreme (hereditary) ruler made a rather shrewd bargain with a credit firm and permitted the territory to be absorbed into the wider firm-and-council jurisdiction, a kind of victory was achieved. A certain kind of organised irrationality came to an end and a different system for the management of human endeavour along vastly more democratic, rational, and equal terms reached its fullest expression. There are some who may find it fitting that the final victory of Firm-based social organisation was secured against a kind of autocratic monarchy whose claim to legitimacy of rule may offer an extreme variation of the vagaries of irrational politicraft, but the King of Eswatini was by no means the most extreme variant of internal contradictions and absurdities of his form of social organisation. His claim to represent the interests of his 'nation' was significantly more well grounded than many of the more 'legitimate' 'democracies' whose dissolution his kingdom watched with perhaps some justifiable schadenfreude. In the terms of the 'nation-state' mythos, the King of Eswatini was entirely legitimate, and his form of social organisation far more in keeping with the entities in the minds of poets and statespersons who coined the term than perpetually anxious entities like 'The United Kingdom' or the 'United States of America', preoccupied as they were in their respective periods of terminal decline with notions of what it meant to be 'British' or 'American'. A UniPrep student can almost instantly discredit the kind of arguments that filled newspapers and books for decades in this sad, disordered period of human history. Of course, the very term "nation-state", to contemporary ears, offers perhaps its most damning condemnation, a judgment it is difficult not to share upon even a cursory perusal of its record as all the aspects of political and social advance that are now understood to support healthy and sustainable development will evidence. For all its pathologies, however, the nation-state was surprisingly durable, and a serious student of politicraft must pose the question of how something so patently dysfunctional could have endured so long. Thus, in the production of a textbook on Firm Balance Politicraft, it is necessary to begin by looking to the past in an attempt to understand how certain prevailing wisdoms came to be. The novice reader will quickly see that far from being the 'natural' state of human organisation, rationality in politicraft requires a kind of permanent vigilance. Today we are not smarter than those who came before us, but, one must hope, we have learned the lessons of their failures. Politicraft as a social science is based on this proposition.

In the time that attended the rise of the nation-state, intense sanguinary conflicts were the rule, and for more than a century, seething, unresolved and irreconcilable incoherencies at the heart of the global governance system threatened the survival of the entire human race, and even the biosphere itself. Such conflicts regularly centred on bizarre, accidental circumstances, like in which nation-state's territory certain natural resources were located. Many may be superficially familiar with such events by reading satirical writers of recent decades who have chosen wars centred around the most destructive 'resource' of all, petroleum, to lampoon the ridiculous and bizarre foibles of previous ages, but the historian of the period will become grimly familiar with the deadly earnest in which these conflicts were fought. Those reading the work of Habib al-Jadid in UniPrep schools, as is now common, may laugh out loud at his merciless satires skewering the endlessly venal and incompetent regime that misruled the former United States of America at the beginning of this century as it conducted its misadventures in his native country of Iraq, but those familiar with the history will regard him as among the most bone-dry of wits. Well aware that the fundamental rule of a satirist's art is to keep a work within the bounds of plausibility, al-Jadid invariably left out many of the crucial facts in his raucous tetralogy of novels because he knew the inclusion of more facts would strain readers' credulity at his fiction. Can we imagine a world in which weapons of unimaginable destructive capacity are brought to bear on a vastly smaller and less powerful territory for the sole purpose of securing a 'resource' that will poison the planet itself? Sadly, imagination is not the faculty that is required, merely the ability to accept the mind's capacity to believe what suits it in a given moment. The nation-state may no longer exist, but it is never far from becoming the future as well as the past.

Today, farces about the nation-state's international failings are commonplace enough, but the internal history of these curious emanations of the human political psyche must be regarded as singular tragedies. In many self-styled 'advanced' states, a person's opportunities in life could be delimited, even determined entirely, by random physical characteristics, or, more bizarrely still, the physical location of one's birth within certain regions of the political suzerainty of a given nation-state! The idea that an enterprising person interested in working for one of the Firms would be prevented from doing so, or be restricted to living in any given region or zone where a suitable branch office can be found is almost too absurd to contemplate. Nevertheless, this was the world for our ancestors, and that world, we are sporadically reminded, is often terrifyingly proximal. Many of us will recall incidents from our working life, or views espoused by members of the Contestant Class on game shows, wherein we encounter views that are astonishingly retrogressive. Today, we can confidently expect that such relics of perishing psychologies will be excluded, de-credited, and continuously monitored for backsliding. While there is, no doubt, some degree of compulsion in these approaches, one must weigh this against what preceded it: to give even the smallest of concessions to this mindset puts a polity on the road to the 'nation-state trap' as politicraft scientists have come to term the phenomenon. Once a polity begins down this primrose path, incidents like the Cascadian Secession are all but inevitable at the cost of life and productivity. The present geo-economic settlement is far from perfect, but it is at least one that begins from a premise of equality rather than motivated notions of "liberty".

It is with the bleak irony with which professional historians become increasingly acquainted over a career studying the past that one may note that the instrument of today's greatest advancement and human liberation was once the engine of our ancestors' misery and confusion. I presume every reader of this text will know that I am speaking of the joint-stock corporation. The corporation, one shall be forced to admit, was born in a kind of sin, many abuses were carried out in its name. Many lives were, indeed, sacrificed so that it could grow. Nonetheless, I would contend, and my esteemed co-editors, co-authors, and researchers in this volume would surely agree, that the abuses and brutalities that characterised the rise of the corporation and then the Firms were a direct result of the resistance to its rise by the apologists for, and foot soldiers of, the 'nation-state'. While a corporation may be faulted for imperfection, it can at least be understood as progressing toward something better with a robust capacity for self-correction. The utopia of the nation-state can only inspire repugnance in the hearts of the civilised. One may puzzle over the ferocity with which it was fought for by its partisans as the Firms came to administer more and more of the earth. One may remember particularly violent resistance in the southern and western territories of the former United States, and bizarre Masada-esque episodes involving esoteric cults in remote territories such as the Falkland Islands, but the ultimate defeat of the nation-state was essentially a kind of recognition, a sense that it was what historians in an earlier period called a "god that failed" and that administration by firms was both inevitable but also more in keeping with historical forms of political organisation, many of which served as greater guarantors of peace and good governance than the nation-states that replaced them. One may look to the maligned period that immediately preceded the rise of the nation-state, the deliberately misnamed "Dark Ages" in the history books of the nation-state period, the age roughly extending from the fall of the Western Roman Empire to the bleak loser's Peace of Westphalia. Feudalism is the name generally given to the primary social organisational form of this time period in Europe, a complex, highly functional and subtly democratic system which, while scarred somewhat by unjust hierarchies and an over-reliance on superstition and conscious mystification, nevertheless managed to provide the dim outline for our contemporary period.

To describe the present age as a kind of feudalism is in no way to disparage it. Planners have devised highly effective methodologies for managing the lacunae previous iterations of feudal organisation threw up. My collaborators and I hope that this textbook will provide you with a sense of the underlying structure of the open, self-organising governance - to use an antique term - 'model' that defines global commerce and social policymaking. We also hope to offer a glimpse of the lived experience of people in various corners of the globe living under different, but connected, social orderings. The free flow of ideas is crucial to any functioning social system, and we hope that our textbook will offer food for thought both on the realities that guide policymaking, but also areas where improvements could be made. We hope a generation of hungry political minds will use the frameworks and strategies described herein, and the comprehensive social portrait they endeavour to provide, to address the challenges of the present, but also eras to come, in which history, at its best, can provide a toolkit for understanding the future. As any junior worker in a Firm understands, our fate is what we make of it. Let us all endeavour to make a fate worthy of the world we have inherited.

Welcome to cLIMB. We're here to help you find yourself. Maybe you're looking to find new work. Maybe you're looking for the right tools for the right job. Maybe you're looking for that special someone. Maybe you're looking for all of the above (and more to boot!). Whatever it is you're trying to find, we can help. With our special NowCast technology, you can fit yourself into a role at one of the top Firms, one of the best Unis, or try your luck against legendary Contestants of the past on their own turf. Here at **cLIMB** we provide you with a fully realised digital space to match your ambitions and we populate it with REAL WORLD DATA to offer the most realistic and honest experience possible.

You want to work for EngelChevco investment energy? We can put you wherever you think you'll fit, in the field, on the swap floor, even in the corner office. For a competitive fee, we can send an impression of your experience to the Firm of your choice.

You've heard of Data Dating? Well, we can take you to the next level. So you've met someone you like, and you know you really like them, what will it be like when/if that Special Moment comes? No need to be anxious. **cLIMB** can help you find answers.

If you're looking for a way up, what are you waiting for?
cLIMB aboard!

**all constructions reflect the best data modelling available on the date of issue, and are not to be understood as a faithful reproduction of any experience offered. Special Moment impression transfers subject to council and Firm-based restrictions. All age restrictions in your Firm jurisdiction will apply for applications.*

Friend Dealer

They're very careful now. They know how to find the fakes. That's why you have to come to someone who knows what they're doing. That's why you have to be careful, too. That's why you have to pay. Anyone who tells you they can do it for free is lying or incompetent. Probably both. Certainly both.

In the abstract, there was nothing wrong with my previous friends. Not as friends, per se, I mean. They were mostly people I'd been hanging out with for years in the city, back before things got so serious. People I grew up with. People I knew from my course at Uni. People I met at work. People I loved. But, if you're going down a certain road, there's a moment when you have to choose. You can try putting it off, but you can't put it off forever. If you do, someone else will make the decision for you. They'll see what you value, and value you accordingly. Someone is the wrong word. It's all done by machine, by algorithm. When I was growing up, I remember people saying it was 'inhuman', but now that I'm living in it, I can't imagine anything more human. The algorithm is us. We train it. We feed it. We live with it. We are the ones it performs for. It's for us. It is us. For better and for worse. Friends are the hardest thing. The other elements aren't easy, but at least they can be understood. Cred sorting. Occupancy renewal requirements. Production quotas. All of that can wear on your mind, but it's all logical. It's all rational. It's how you build a functioning society. It's how you keep the governments from coming back. The friend stuff, though, it takes something out of you. One day you look your friends in the eye for the last time. You know it. They know it. You make the best. It's what people do.

They understood. Most of them did. Between us, I couldn't let them all go. I keep a few of them on a separate phone. I paid for them to have separate phones for me, too. It was the least I could do.

You have to be moving. Growing. Upgrading. The terms of social service are forever changing. You have to show you're moving in the right direction, if you want to keep moving in the right direction. The only way to show that you're moving in the right direction is to speak in the language they understand, and it's a very difficult one. Often the words aren't what matters, but the syntax, the way things fit together, the way relationships balance each other, the way they create legibility for the system. Friends are important. They're a 'tell'. They tell you who you are, and they tell other people who you are. Or who you think you are. Or if you think about who you are. When you're trying to get hired, when you're moving flats, when you're trying to get a loan, they're looking. They're looking at everything about you. What you do, what you buy, whom you buy it for. What you don't buy. The further you go, the harder it gets, the more scrutiny that comes for you, but you can't stop, you can't settle. Not really. You can, but stopping sends a signal that it's ok to forget you. I'm not ready to be forgotten, not yet at least.

You'll hear different opinions, some say it's freer now than before. Some say it's less free. The one group says we've overcome the irrationalities, that we're finally able to be honest about the things that drive progress. We've shed the past, the prejudices, we live in the truth now. The truth hurts sometimes, but pain is another word for growth. You always have to remember that. The other group, they say that we have made progress. That Firms are a lot more reasonable than governments ever were, but that there are new problems that didn't exist before. These people talk a lot about 'privacy' and how it's supposed to be this magic formula that allows you to solve your problems on your own terms or discover some deep, underlying self that The Firms don't want you to find. I don't really follow their logic, but the friend thing, it kind of shows they aren't completely crazy.

The way someone explained it to me when I started at Silverado was that the friend thing was a kind of unspoken component of our lives as data. No one, not even the more ruthless Firms, could admit that they checked up on stuff like that, but everyone knew they did and you'd be stupid not to optimise your friend situation when and wherever possible. Everyone knows that most of the friends you'll have, you know, *organically*, will be people you grew up with or went to school with. And they know where you went to school, obviously. And that creates a barrier. But there is space; there are cracks. If you're not born into Management, you have to master the task of finding these cracks, maybe even finding places where there are tensions and you can create cracks, if you push that little bit.

'If you're serious about a career here, you have to think about what that means. Think about it, David, everyone in the upstairs offices, they have a model of what an executive looks like, acts like, lives like. What the social life of an executive allows and doesn't allow. You have to be on your toes, 24/7, have every base covered. Friends matter.'

'It all just seems, I don't know, a little bit superficial.'

'On the contrary, it's all about what's going on below the surface. Look, think about how we talk about it, right? You 'make' friends with someone. The way it works at this level is there's just a little bit more emphasis on the "making" bit. I can give you the number of somebody who can help you if you need it. Just ask.'

The algorithm they use is smart. You can drive yourself mad trying to second guess it. Take the school thing. Like I said, if you have a lot of friends from school, that can be a good thing, but so can pricing up, finding new friends who are good and leaving the old, less good, ones behind. But length of friendship itself is clearly a factor in the evaluation system. So if you're constantly making and breaking friendships, that could be like quitting a job too soon after taking it. That might suggest you're not loyal, or that there's something wrong with *you*. They might think your other friends chose to leave you behind. If you're advancing, and you start moving your life around to suit it, you can't let it become too obvious that's what you're doing. You have to balance it. Every step has to be measured and offset so it isn't clear that you're just angling to improve your data. In this situation that means you should always definitely keep some people from your friends, the good ones - the ones that you *know* are good - but if you leave too many of the less good ones behind too soon, or, crucially, if you leave them as a group all at once, then they can kind of sense you're gaming and you're finished. The crack you think you're creating gives way, and you fall into the icy water below. You're gone. As I say, all this thinking, it's maddening.

Moving up, finding something good, it's important. If you don't you could get lost too. I had a friend a year ago, we worked for the same company, he had some health issues, nothing major but he had to go in for a series of treatments. He couldn't keep up with the payments now that the NHS is long gone - it had its upsides even if it was as inefficient as they all say it was, I've read about it. That friend I knew, though, he's had three jobs since he missed those medical payments. Each one was less senior than the previous. I lost touch with him a while back. I kind of had to. I don't know what he's up to now, but the last I'd heard, he was thinking of going full Contestant Class to try to win enough to get to zero. Such a huge, humiliating step. Falling like that after all his education and the years he's spent working his way up. I feel for him. But he could have been a bit more careful. Don't get me wrong, you obviously can't blame someone for something like that, a health issue - though there are companies now that can offer you predictive health programmes for reasonable prices; information is power. Still, I can't help but think he could have been better prepared. It wasn't the health thing so much, more that he didn't have a bigger, better masterplan. He'd been in his job for five years doing more or less the same role. He could have kept trying to move forward, into something real, something good. What happened to him was really a wake up call for me; that, and the thought that some day it might be worth seeking a partnership and kids. I wasn't going to be anybody's SwipeMate when they divided my age by my earnings as it was, that's for sure. The choice was clear, I had to level up. And I wasn't going to be able to do that by myself.

Once you've figured out where you want to go, what you want to do, and to be, then you have to plot out a good pathway. Make clear signposts for yourself so you can say, 'OK, we're at a new level, now. We need to reassess how everything fits together, how *everyone* fits together.' Once you've got a path, you have to test it. Test your luck: apply for a job you know you wouldn't have got before. See if you can get wait-listed for a flat you might (or might not) be able to afford. There are signals; you have to tune into their frequency, listen for the delicate, obscure music they produce. They're the sounds that hold the world together. If you're satisfied that your pathway is working for you, then you can get serious, in fact, you have to get serious. You have to be prepared to talk to a pro. Luckily I had a friend, someone good. He put me in touch with someone to sort me out, and that was how I got Michael's number. Michael's not his real name.

I texted him. He was very cagey at first. A lot of 'Who's this?' and 'Who gave you this number?' but I told him I was Silverado, and that got him talking. Eventually we managed to get a real conversation going. Michael said he couldn't just take me on. He'd have to vet me first. There was an upfront fee, he told me, instead of the free consultation I'd been promised.

'It's been a while since I worked with your friend Duncan. He's a good chap, but he's got the old figures. Haven't got a choice. They're tightening things up. You know how it is, you have to keep moving upwards, no? Anyway, friend, I assure you, I'm worth every Coin."

I didn't like paying extra, but he was telling the truth. There are lots of risks. Dealing is technically illegal, and so he'd be facing serious fines if they ever nicked him. And they do get Dealers once in a while, and they make examples out of them, bar them even from Contestant Class roles. They have to be assigned jobs, and they're never fun, and they're never in good places, out on the dunes of the old cities Lost Angeles and Lost Vegas, or they put them in the sweatboxes. Everybody knows they can't actually stop the dealing, though, not with things the way they are. The price of changing the system is never worth the advantage a few people get gaming it. And there are plenty of people who do it, from the demand and the supply side. There's always an incentive somewhere for someone to either slip Dealers information about the algorithms. Or sometimes there's a flaw somewhere in the encryptions that a smart Dealer can break. Michael sent me a few of his clients' accounts to look through. It was impressive.

One afternoon while I was having my lunch blip in Silverado's green enclosure, I got a message from an account using Amharic script. I knew it was Michael. I changed the language setting and used the frequency analysis key he posted me weeks ago when he took me on. It was good news. He had a portfolio for me to look through. The bill was attached. I'd have to pay some shadow company with a Cook Islands address. SoftCoin preferred.

I looked over his dossier. It was really impressive. Everyone earned more than me, except for a few people linked to our Council. Tradeoffs, I suppose, but, on the whole, a masterclass in friend sourcing. Apparently, just from what he told me when he was explaining the process, Michael's company does all the data mining itself, modelling you, your life, your projection, and figuring out who would be the best and most plausible friends you could make. The backstory bit isn't easy. There were a lot of surprises, I remember one time when we chatted about 'face-to-faces' with the new friends.

'I think there's a mistake in your pricing. Face-to-face is listed as cheaper than online interactions.'

'It's not a mistake.'

'No?'

'No. What can I say, some of the top tier clients, they don't get out very much, particularly the Council types. It's kind of a side-hustle that technically isn't part of the service. I drop in a few genuinely pleasant chaps in among the Climbers. They tip well if I introduce them to someone they actually like. Take it as a compliment that this service is available for you.'

I did take it that way. Michael gave me a deal on three friends who do regular face-to-faces who had top five percentile ratings on his system. One, Madeleine, works at a mutual. She's great but she drinks a lot more than me. Keeping up with her, it's not easy, but you have to try. Otherwise she'll taunt you. Jad works on some kind of distributed ledger contract thing I don't entirely understand despite the fact that it's all he seems to want to talk about. Cyril works as a Council Drone Liaison. I meet each of them once a month, alternate Third Days. We have a few drinks, sometimes we go for dinner when the pandemic alert levels are low. Mostly they talk, I listen. It involves a lot of travel, and they always want to take driverlesses. Sometimes it's hard work, but then that's what friendship is, really, it's hard work.

Darla, Berlin 29
design/logistics/education/performance artist (Capricorn Sun, Gemini Moon, Scorpio rising - if that matters!)

Highly Educated (MA, Comparative Literature, Harvard University (Abu Dhabi Campus)) Runner, proud tattooed dog mom. Not sure what I'm doing here, I know I want to meet like minded people. Ambition is Critical as they say in Swansea (Not from, but I've been. Ipswich Diva, lived in 8 Firm Jurisdictions, have sooo many stories! Bet you can't wait to hear!). Gym buddies welcome, need someone to send me holo-streams (musics, lects, whatever keeps yr drone buzzing). Up for collabs of all sorts. Business, creative, lurrrve. My story: Guess I see myself as a spiritual entrepreneur, interested in mind-body-biome connections and the ways these flow into markets. Markets are power, I read loads. Tamer ben Ami is FASCINATING (CAPITAL F), how the mind and Firm Logics join up. Do contests once in a while for fun, but NOT a Contestant. I have ten toes so I dip them in many pools and keep one hand free for rosé. Would love to start a major project with the right partner (nudge nudge, wink wink). Could talk about it all night. And probably will! Silly but serious. Drinks are on you until you look like your profile holo. Keep it clean, chaps. No dick pics. Send memes and holo-streams!

#Gym. #Culture #Travel #Workflow #musics #design #mindware #grabadrink

Contestant Classes

People complain. They always do. There's always something wrong. This is bad. This is terrible. Look, I'm the first to say that things aren't perfect, but the thing is, I read a lot of history. It's kind of a hobby of mine. Just read a really interesting book, more politics than history, but it went into the way things were before, back in the day. Really digging into how we got here and why. I'd say, when you consider the big picture - the big and the small picture, really - things are a lot fairer now than before. There are people who say bad things about being a Contestant - it's precarious, it's a racket, it's all fixed, it's oppressive, anyone could do it, that sort of thing. I appreciate that some people are speaking from ignorance. They've never been Contestants. They think it's all misery all the time, 'oh no, am I going to lose and have to live in the outlands? Not even a show trailer bunk to my name?' Admittedly, that can be scary, there are risks, but every day is a risk. Any given time you cross the street you could get run over, and if it's a driverless - especially one with a VPN - your family might not even get compensation. Those things are crazy, I mean how do they still let you have a VPN on your driverless? I guess when you're an Innovator, you can do anything you want to. I've never met an Innovator. I could, I guess, if I went on *Predatorium* and pitched some business idea, but I don't have a business idea. Not sure I'd take it to them if I did. The name 'Predatorium' doesn't exactly suggest they play by the rules. Rules! Sorry, I was supposed to be talking about being a Contestant. Sorry. I guess what I mean is that, as a Contestant, there can be issues, risks, dangers, whatever, but if you stay in the system, like you don't give up just because you lose on a couple of shows, and especially if you're compelling, you're not gonna starve. As long as you're on some show - and there are so, so many shows now - you at least can count on at least some per diem creds - or carpe diem creds, as my agent calls it. The diversity of people you meet as a contestant, for me that's really awesome. That's one of the great things about the New Model, I think. Before, like in the time I read about in that history book, there were only a few shows that gave people a chance to break through, and most of them were horrible and abusive, people eating spiders or having their sex lives filmed and specced on. You can still find shows like that now, of course, but you'd never see one on one of the mainstream channels. Those shows are for freaks now - maybe they always were - voyeurs, spec addicts or hollowsouls. I can't believe stuff like *Prison Pinball* and *Cut Adrift on The Hudson* were some of the top rated shows once upon a time, you look back and you can start to believe the past is another dimension completely, orbiting a different sun. I've only known the period when the shows have been based on skill, physical challenges, mental challenges, ethical challenges, genuinely wholesome content for the most part, and if you want to break through, there are hundreds of opportunities now, thousands, really, maybe tens of thousands. I get offers on my phone for new channel subscriptions every day. I literally can't count them all. Every one of them needs Contestants. And that's just in my own Firm-sector area's production; if you're good with languages that opens up a whole world of other markets to you, too. It can be difficult, and there's a learning curve, I'll admit that, but I'd say, if you were born into the Contestant Classes like I was, your chances are actually better today than they would have been before.

So let's see, what got me interested in history? I got interested, really, when I was a kid. My parents signed me up for the kids' trivia shows, and I got on one straightaway. The education incubators the companies provide were excellent, and that was when I learned about what the historians call Early Reality. To me, it just sounded like a bunch of barbarians ran the world. The thing I keep coming back to that really symbolises it is that there were countries, major ones with big economies, where you could actually die if you couldn't afford to go to a hospital. People were literally afraid of going to the hospital because they'd get into debt and there weren't any easy ways to burn off debt like there are now with Cross-Generational Hiring and that kind of thing. From what I understand, the guys who started *Happy Organ*, which is probably still the most popular show on MedView, got their idea from what they'd learned about that period of history. I can totally see how they came up with it. If you watch old news clips from Early Reality on the nostalgia channels, you can find out about people who had to do fundraisers and things for treatments or transplants, or they had to rely on some random person donating an organ, or whatever, to them. If you think about it, basically it already was a TV show, but you only found out it was like that after the story had concluded. There was all the suffering, all the high-stakes, life-or-death stuff, but none of the actual drama or resolution that makes shows like *Happy Organ* so good. Basically it was all just totally random, disorganised, violent and bleak. No matter how good your narrative was, whether you were compelling or just a normal person, you couldn't count on anyone helping you, you just had to hope that maybe someone might see your health fundraiser and kick in some money! And the weirdest thing was they had creds back then, but they didn't give them to everyone, they only gave them to people with money. Thankfully now there are so many medical shows, that you practically can't go wrong no matter what your issue is. There's always some way to get treatment without paying up front. Sure, sometimes patients die on the medical shows - not *Happy Organ* of course, how off brand would that be! - but even then, the spec returns from the Funds on secondary markets go to the patient's family, so they're looked after either way, and it can soften the blow of the loss.

Maybe I'm a little biased. Like I said, I was born in the Contestant Classes. My parents were Contestants, too. And my grandparents. My mum and dad met during auditions for shows. Mum was trying to get on *DromoDancers*, that old endurance dancing show, and my dad was a contestant on *One Shot*, the show where you turn up and someone punches you and if you don't get knocked down, you advance to the next week and get a cred prize. Most contestants barely make it one episode. My dad was on it for a year. You could say I'm proud. *One Shot* isn't really so popular anymore, it was kind of one of the last of the old school shows. I think it linked competition and violence too much, and some campaign groups got it relegated to late-night screenings, and then to the gore channels. It's still on, but my dad never mentions he was a champ. It's not really his life now. He lives in the Costa del Sol Council region. He's one of the few Contestants living in his village. Would people look down on him if they knew? Some might, but other people would be fascinated, I'd bet. Anyone want to bet? A little future speccing? I'm digressing, sorry, I know this is meant to be a short essay, but the point is that the contestant classes have always felt totally natural, even ideal to me. I'm on my fifth show now since I was seven, when they let you start competing officially - of course all Contestants are born competing, so the fact that you can finally make Coins feels like you've already been given a prize. I know that there is some prejudice about us. And people who've had to change classes do resent it. I know they look down on us. It's not all their fault. Their schools - they still call them "schools" to appeal to tradition or whatever, not EdIncs like I went to or UniPreps as they're officially known - they train them to regard us as somehow stupider or weaker than them, like it's our fault we're Contestants. Like we did something. News flash, people: we do *everything*! They think that way about us because they know that if they fall into the Contestant Class and turn up on some show, people who they knew and grew up around will look at them the way they look at us, or maybe worse because they know that they fell. Fell? Wow, there I am doing it too. It's in the language. You 'fall' into the Contestant Classes. You 'rise' to Management Class. You 'Sublime' - always capitalised - into being an Innovator. We, Contestants, 'aspire' to PMC status - 'Pre-Management Class'. It's all so stupid. They say the classes are good for us. Class consciousness breeds competition. They say it all the time, in the EdIncs; I'm sure in the schools, too. As for me, I think you 'land' in the Contestant Class personally, because there's all kinds of territory to conquer here. I think I'd find it boring in the Management Classes, or as a Hired, sounds to me like you just do the same thing all day, every day, until the sun finally sets on you.

But I know it's not easy landing here if you weren't born this way. A couple of years ago, I was on *Perfect Pitches*, the show where you write a song that sums up your new business proposal - I was good at the song bit, not the proposal bit - and there were some contestants who'd been pre-managers but who had a stroke of bad luck. Their flat came up on *Mobile Homes* and got lost from under them while they were studying. They weren't really prepared. They just got a letter one day saying that their house's number had come up in the *Mobile Homes* Lottery and they were going to have to defend their property, select a specialist subject and the crew would be around in two weeks to film. I guess they didn't know their house was a private let, which is weird because almost all university properties are private lets. I guess they didn't really know how the world worked. Their parents sheltered them. I can understand it. You want your PMC kids to believe the people at the top got there by merit, or skill, or something, not just luck and a high tolerance for boredom. Anyway, when the day came to film on *Mobile Homes*, they screwed up on the questions and the challenger won. He got to keep their flat, like always. That was just the start of the bad news, their landlord, who they'd been trying to reach for the two weeks before their appearance, found out about it eventually, after the fact, and sued them for negligence. They got a very unsympathetic judge - former Contestant Class it turned out, I looked him up - and they ended up having to leave their courses and most of them ended up joining the Contestant Classes to try to find a new place to live, and to pay their landlord off for losing his house.

The one I spoke to most on *Perfect Pitches*, Amy, she was pretty bitter.

'It's not fair. We had no idea. We tried to find our landlord. We did everything right!'

Pure Pre-Manager mentality. *It's not fair. We played by the rules. We deserve better!* It's the first lesson you learn as a Contestant: you can do everything right and still lose. The game picks its winners. When it goes wrong, the only thing you can do is sign up tomorrow for the next show. There's always a next show. Of course, all those ex-students got crushed on *Perfect Pitches*. They were up against experienced Contestants, and they were still in a kind of shell shock, like they'd witnessed something impossible, a person turning into an eagle, that kind of thing. I laughed along with all the other Contestants when they played their stupid song to the judges, but I couldn't help feeling sorry for them inside. They knew so little, and they were already into their twenties. Management drifting a little further out from them every day into the mist. I've seen other pre-managers in green rooms in the years since. They're always like that first batch, panicked, fearful like wild animals waking up in a cage, unsure of how much deeper the tunnel they see themselves falling into reaches. There are times when I feel like I'd like to reach out to them, to show them that there's a lot to love about competing, a lot to learn too, and you don't even have to pay creds to a university; here, competition is free. I want to tell them that there's beauty here, growth, hope, if they'll just allow themselves to see it. I want to say these things, but I never do. I know they wouldn't listen. They're too busy saying the same thing to themselves, over and over: 'I'm not really here. I'm not really here.'

You've heard of VaperCore.
You've heard of Goblinstep.
You've heard of WitchWave.
You've heard of Gin'gaTrap.
You've heard of WretchTech.
You've heard of POPverty.
You've heard of Brexhaust.
You've heard of XXXtractFlex.

Now experience DethDrill.

Check the new release from Sanctus Waves Files: *Ice Flow,* by Pale Flairz. Five years in the making, thousands of algorithms deep, Ice Flow takes you into a world of absolute sonic dys-nature. Drone-fire synths quadruple tap on beats that hit hard enough to shiver new tectonic plates into existence. Deeper than the iron deposits inside Planet 1 itself, Ice Flow forges a totally unique set of narratives genn'd by the life Pale Flairz has lived, the people she's known, and the smack-and-stack life of a hustler on the way up the rungs. Slip into the deadwaters of '$ludgeLyf3', or scream it out with 'No Specc Dexie'. Ice Flow has tracks for office hours and overtime. Through the course of seventy-eight lobe-crushing tracks, Ice Flow moves from the propulsive dance-floor rhythms of XXXtractFlex to the deeply introv ruminations of WretchTech, along the way birthing an entirely new musical genre: DethDrill, mining out the most crystalline specimens of DethVibe's punishing riffs and smelting them into the cold, spacey atmospheres of SpaceDrill. Get down with GhostSwag's latest creation before the world turns. Get the max from Ice Flow before we find out what life after DethDrill sounds like. Free Neural upload with promotion code.

www.SanctusWaves.co.in.

Includes the singles, 'Off Dem BrontoRibz', 'K-Ron', and the smash hit, 'InnerDolphinGod'.

MindStream Inc.

First we sacked the writers. That was the easy part. We barely had to pay them anyway. Then we sacked the editors, and that was a little harder. Our editors had made their bones during the Reality period, so tonnes of experience. It was sad to say good-bye, but the numbers were healing-crystal clear: we were better off without them. I've been in the business a long time, but it was a new thing for me: developing content without writers and editors, it felt wrong somehow, but in the end everybody at the Firm understood that if we weren't prepared to take the plunge, then we didn't really believe in our product. How could we sell it to clients if we didn't believe it ourselves? Sometimes you just have to start moving your wings and trust that you'll be able to fly. Trust is a grand thing, of course, but every acrobat trains with a net. For the first six months we worked with an agency just in case, belt and braces and all that. We kept a pool of independent contractors on zero hours in the event we needed a bit of help somewhere along the line. Happily, we never even had to make an enquiry call.

That was the creative side, which, in a way, was the easy part. The brass were more than happy to be rid of the writers, and they trusted us enough when we told them we were sacking the editors to keep investing. Though there were some raised eyebrows, and when you've seen some of the eyebrows this lot have, well, don't get me started…

The real challenge, where we started getting serious pushback, came when we had our quarterly conference call and we were trying to convince the brass that we could do without crews and logistics people. Carey from PaterNoster Capital, in particular, he was very skeptical. He kept cutting me off:

'I don't see how you can make a high quality production without a production team.'

'That's just the point though, Carey, we're *not* the producers. We—'

'If you're not the producers what are we investing in *you* for?'

'You're paying us *not* to be the producers. You're paying so no one "produces" in the sense you mean ever again.'

Got a bit quiet then. Tight, that call was, but I was able to talk them round. Showed them the projections. Fair bit of harrumphing, but I think curiosity was enough to keep them online. Carey stuck around, too, all credit to/from him - little VC joke there - maybe he just wanted to see if we fell flat. Maybe he had a short position on us too, who knows? Water through the turbine now, as they say. Of course we didn't fall flat, and he's a much richer person for it, as thankfully, we all are. As I say, the skepticism I understood, at least to some degree. We were working at the absolute fringe, the frontier of content. We were building the bridge we were walking across, as the saying runs, but our investors all had sufficient appetite for risk, and I'm happy to say that after that first year we saw that they were all well-fed. It was the distribution companies we partnered with initially that were the most resistant. They were media people, not VCs or Firms, lots of them with fancy UniGradPasses and stuff, convinced that they knew what made people sit and watch content: plot, rising action, climax, falling action, three acts, stories with conflicts and resolution, hero's journey.... all that rubbish. I remember one meeting where we just showed a distributor some vlogs from EyeTube to explain to him that yes, there was a market, thank you very much, a lucrative one at that, and we were the next logical step in it. The poor bloke didn't get it at all.

'People watch this shit?'

Of course they do, fella. Of course they do. People will watch anything if you give them the chance. I was stunned they didn't already know that. We showed them the subscription numbers, the advertising revenues. They got religion pretty quickly, as the saying goes.

As for the science bit - I suppose that's where the magic happens, as they say - well, it's not my strong suit. I'm a maths guy up to a point, but when people start talking about experiment design and things like that, I admit, my eyes do glaze over. But even glazed, they're eyes that can see an opportunity, a real one, when it comes along. Everyone has a story, that's the curse of content creation. Everyone has a story and they're bloody hell for leather to tell it, and to tell me they want me - or rather CharlesGainesMedia - to tell it. I probably get four thousand emails a day. The system weeds out at least two-thirds, but I do eyeball the rest, once the keyword filters have done their thing. I knew there was something different when I got the message from the team at MindForge Imaging lab. The lead researcher, Elvira, was the one who messaged me.

> *Hello Charles,*
>
> *I hope you're doing well in these uncertain times. I wanted to present some findings from a research project that we feel could change the face of contemporary entertainment. Needless to say, CharlesGainesMedia are leaders in the field, and we trust our project will offer new opportunities for rapid market capture.*

Too right! Well, as I say, she had my attention, but every plonker out there with a wifi connection and a university email address thinks they've invented the ultimate killer app. You could paper the walls of your house - or my house at least - in all the peer review journals that churn out what amounts to bad advertising copy, so I was cautious. I presented the email to my own team down in RD&D and I could see the Britpound signs appearing in people's eyes. I sent Vikram down to their labs to investigate the claims, to drill down a bit, as they say. He's the only one of us in the office with an actual applied science background. He did cognition science - something to do with brains, at least - at Cambridge. He was the right person for the job. So bloody thorough. He took the driverless to Reading where their lab is and in an hour of his arrival, here's what he wrote me:

Afternoon, Charles (et al.),

Good news: I think we won't miss my driverless fare. Came to the lab. Sitting in their shit commissary now. At any rate, the skinny: I assumed it was bullshit, of course; they're academics after all, why wouldn't it be? Let them give me their pitch. Was amazed how slick it all was. Weren't just a lot of Lab Coat Larrys. Showed me the whole process, and a couple of papers they'd published on direct-mind-imaging (DMI) as they call it. Looked pretty legit on first glance. Actual numbers. Not the usual wishes dressed as research. So I said, 'OK. Looks fab. Can you do it to me?'. They looked at each other, and the woman in charge, this Elvira you corresponded with, smiles and says, 'As long as you sign this release form, we'd be delighted.' Release was a nice touch. Said they could use any footage generated for promotional purposes, etc.. I was eligible for a one-off payment, but no mechanical royalties or anything like that. If they were charlatans, they were charlatans with a decent legal team. Fair play. They put the stuff on me, all the VR stuff, that is. Was well designed. Comfortable. Better than most earbuds at least. Then the images are supposed to come up on a screen as it reads your thoughts. Thought it was probably just old carnival stuff, mind-reader tricks and priming effects, etc.. So I just started thinking about fruit. Just fruit and nothing else, and soon enough, there it was on the screen, the plum I thought of, the peach, then the quince, which I threw in to really push it. Tech worked. At least it was working well enough to sign a contract for a half year. I'll let you look over it to finalise things.

See you tonight,
V.

That was two years ago. Elvira's on our board here now. There were some teething issues. Mostly interface. We had to get the helmet size down, lighter weight, smoother look, and, at first, finding subscribers was a little delicate, but I knew it was going to work. I had an instinct about MindGames, just a feeling that people would click with it. We're still early days but the numbers speak for themselves. I mean, it is kind of obvious when you think about it, people always want to know what's happening in other people's minds. What's going on under the bonnet, as they say- possibly literally, maybe, if you're the sort who wears a bonnet, and if you do, fair play to you. We focus-grouped it in some pubs in Deptford, mostly kids, but they loved it. The focus group stuff we did later, with the general market, was a little inconclusive, people were wary, but once we started testing younger people the uptake looked a lot more reassuring. For me, I think we really achieved lift off when we took the plunge and did a round of free subscriptions for influencers. Paid a load of teenagers 10k for six months to feed the feed, so to speak, for a min of 10 hours. The brass didn't like the price tag, and we had to write some air tight waivers on that one, as you might expect, content warnings and that. I admit, I had a few sleepless nights at the start. I remember lying there in bed, tossing and turning as they say, nothing worked, couldn't shut off, then the thought came to me: Charles, old boy, maybe you should try a dose of your own medicine. So I logged onto the stream. I tuned in to some little oik in Devon with 500,000 followers on SqueakBox. Put me right to sleep. Been sleeping very well indeed ever since.

Of course, it's not the sort of thing you'd have gotten away with before, all the legal niceties and privacy Nazis carping, all living in the old world, the ancient before-time time. But that's mostly gone now, business can actually do what it's supposed to do now. Cracking time to be alive if you ask me. And 8 million subscribers in the first year would seem to agree. We haven't reached perfection yet, needless to say. We're working through things, some of the bugs. For example, what happens if someone tries to hack a stream? You've got to keep tight control over the server. We've got the opposite problem, too, though: how can our advertisers effectively integrate product placement without losing the integrity of the project's USP? The latter is easier to solve than the former, turns out. Again it was Vikram who came up with the masterstroke: you don't place the product in the source stream, you place it in the *reception* stream. Bish bash! That way you can personalise the advert and maximise the revenue stream all without 'tampering' with the source stream. Inspiring, frankly. We've got a long way to go, a lot of growing to do, but I expect we'll have the CircumAtlantic market on lock by the end of the decade. We've got competitors now, too, the ultimate compliment. Capital truly is flowing right now, especially since we finally put the cinema nonces in their place. It's going to be rough and tumble, as they say, along the road ahead, but it's not really a road, it's a stream and we're paddling hard out here in the white water. I'm confident we'll get where we want to. We've got the will, and we've got the bandwidth.

Daventry GreEnclosure

Ten years in the making. Tomorrow is finally here!

At Daventry GreEnclosure, stewardship of our environment is a sacred duty, but it's also an amazing day out. Opening weekend 2078 at Daventry GreEnclosure is now taking bookings. Bring the entire family for an unforgettable adventure in nature. 662.6 km2 of untouched rewilded wilderness, Daventry GreEnclosure is the most expansive NatWorld reserve in the CircumAtlantic region. In the twenty years since there has been a human footprint in the Daventry region, nature has returned. There is no better place to see isle wildlife as nature planned it - for the most part.

Daventry GreEnclosure is proud to announce that its crack team of zoologists were able to locate and tag a huge number of the surviving elephants and giraffes from the former West Midlands Safari Park and create functioning, local habitats for them. They're a little shy so you'll have to book a Premium Experience to hang out with them, but Daventry GreEnclosure can confirm they'd love to make your acquaintance!

But that's not all. In our VisionGlenns you can generate your OWN ecosystem with fully data-mapped animals. In our HistoryHideyHole you can see what it was like when humans walked the grounds of Daventry GreEnclosure.

What are you waiting for? Book now before Opening Weekend is full.

Daventry GreEnclosure is fully biodomed and climate controlled, and fully drone protected within a 100km2 radius. Digital signal restoration available for premium rate (included in VIP packages).

Deals:

Hired Family Day Pass	1000.00
Hired Family Day Pass w/personalised ecosystem	4000.00
VIP Experience Tour	3000.00
VIP Experience Tour with Hunting Privileges (hologram)	7000.00
VIP Experience Tour with Hunting Privileges (IRL)	15000.00
Total Package (includes all access VIP pass, hunting privileges (IRL) and trading rights for resale of kill/commodity and derivative futures gains)	250000.00
Council Support Credit Takers	Please enquire, rates subject to daily change

All prices in Great Britpound, other currencies accepted at day rate at time of park's opening.

Spec Room

You knock on the door, and unless there are plague issues - sometimes even if there are - they let you into the spec rooms. The ones I like aren't the official ones the big companies run. The ones on the high street, Leprechaun Spreads and those places, or even the fancy ones down west in Mayfair. Everyone there is just like me. There, you're supposed to treat it like a sport. You win some, you lose some. It's just entertainment. It's just a game. It might be a game, but what are the stakes? Winning and losing means something different in a speccing room in Mayfair with people speccing with money their ancestors made than it does the rooms up in the Contestant Class urbs where every spec is life and death. If you're serious about speccing, if you love it, if you need it, you have to go to these rooms.

The rooms are easy enough to find. There's no shortage, you just find an alley off a high street in a Contestant district and there will be at least one. I don't really keep up with the laws, they change all the time anyway, but I don't think these places are illegal, and since they stopped with the stupid licensing stuff once the Firms agreed to finally dispense with the pretences about royal prerogative, the biggest obstacle to setting a spec room up is gone. These places, out in the fringe-lands, they're not doing anything particularly shady, but 'respectable' types are thin on the ground there. The atmosphere is just so different, the intensity, the aspirationality. In Contestant spec rooms, things are far more serious. You spec wrong, you're down a week's wages maybe. You spec wrong twice, you might move from Contestant to criminal. It's personal, it's closer to the heart. There's none of the stupid peacocking. Nobody wears a suit. No free cocktails. No stupid James Bond bullshit. Nobody buys a round of drinks if they win. A lot of people aren't even drinking. And Contestants, as you'd expect, know how to compete. It's not like Mayfair or the big Firm places, where people are sitting around tables and leisurely tapping their specs in. If you want to talk about a culture in these places, the word I'd use is 'pungent'. Yelling, screaming, win or lose. Bets are always going off, someone's celebrating, someone's shouting down a phone. There's none of the iron silence like in the big places.

You might say I'm slumming. You might say I work in a Firm, I'm on thousands of Coins a week, what could I possibly have in common with the faces I see in these back alley spec rooms? If you think this kind of stuff, you're thinking about it all wrong. Yeah, I'm a Hired, not a Contestant, but, let's be honest, who knows how long that will last. Every time I come to one of these places, and I can't ever see myself stopping coming, I see what can happen to me, to anyone. There are former Hireds there, always, though they're not a majority. You can tell which ones they are, they're the only ones who look like they aren't having fun. Speccing isn't just an occupation for them, it's a science. They all have systems, and if you're in a spec room that serves alcohol, you will hear about them. They suss me out every time. They know I'm a Hired just by looking at me, maybe it's the haircut, the shave, the way I carry myself. They see all the things that are invisible to any Hired. They pull you to one side, try to make conversation. 'Close one earlier,' or 'hard luck tonight,' that type of thing, but they just want to get you talking so they can tell you about their system.

'Did you ever think about using a system to spec? I have a really good one.'

'How's it working for you tonight?'

'It's not great tonight. OK, but not great.'

'Not much of a system, though, is it, if it doesn't work all the time?'

'You don't get it. No, it's working, it just, it takes a while to work sometimes.'

Then they'll go off for hours talking to you about Poisson Distributions and fractals. The only way to stop it is to walk away. Sometimes they keep talking even after you do. You can hear them between the shouts and groans. These systems, I figured, are the way they tell themselves they're still not really Contestants - or whatever class they're in now - not really. Contestants just turn up and spec. Hireds apply their advanced analytical minds to the problem of speccing. They're Hireds by nature, of course, and they'll be back someday. The system will get them there. If you encounter these types, all you can do is to find a new spec as quickly as possible. They get you in the toilets, at the wash basins. They catch your eye in a mirror. Their hungriness seeps into you if you spend too much time with them. I have a superstition that they actively suck luck out of you. I don't know how it happens, I don't have a system about it, but I think it's true. They suck your luck out but it doesn't go into them, it just floats off like a gas into the room without ever being enough of a dose to make anyone else luckier. Pure loss. They're a hazard, but it's worth it. You see everyone in a Contestant spec room, all of human life. So you can't call it slumming anymore than going to a GreEnclosure is slumming. And it is like a GreEnclosure; it's an ecology. Life teems, overspilling itself. Everything and everyone you see are in the flow, grains of sand blowing back and forth in the desert of luck.

Almost everyone in The Firms specs, but usually it's on the classy trades, dogs, horses, the heritage stuff. But everyone knows that's not the best speccing. They'll say it's seedy, or "ungentlemanly" to spec on the real stuff, the rough stuff, the good rooms specialise in. A good spec makes you feel the stakes inside, like you're what's being specced on and you know it. The rough stuff is where you can really feel. Speccing on weather. Speccing on insurance. BloodBuddy stuff. Everything under the sun and the sun too. Solar flares this year? Maybe. One of the best times I ever had speccing was with Reg from work. He took me to one of the greatest rooms I've ever been to, out in Rayners Lane of all places. We're putting together a little map of all the good Contestant spec rooms, Reg and I, every time he finds them faster than me.

He's out every night. Literally every night. I go out three, four nights a week. The rest of the week I do the usual work function stuff, maybe once in a while I meet someone for a lovegig, but he's literally in a spec room until he has to come to work in the morning. Has suits in his office at the Firm and he either showers in our gym or at the spec room itself. I've seen him do it. That night, the great night, I got a new pin from Reg and I knew he'd found a new place. That place in Rayners could have been anything from the outside, takeaway, hardware shop, church. As it was, the main room was a Sri Lankan restaurant. As always in these places, the food was amazing. Best raita I've ever had. I'd go there even if there weren't speccing in the back, but, of course, there is.

I was blown away with their set up. You'd think you were in one of the high end places down in Park Lane or Portland Square from the tech they have. Every kind of speccing from the over the counter stuff to these crazy boards where names would appear and disappear in seconds. I'd see names blink different colours, sometimes two would come up the same colour and disappear. What in the world was all of this? Reg explained it all to me:

"Yeah, nice, eh? That's a ScoreSettler. You spec on people's credit scores. You can pick a region, or do it globally. The big swings are on the global ones. Sometimes it's too hot for me to touch, but I usually try at least one a night. What I like to do is a double up. That's when you can make them go head to head."

"Them?"

"You pick one, one of those names See? Let's take that one. You put his number into the app and they start showing him credit adverts on his feeds. Then you pick somebody else. That guy, Enrique Maas, let's pick him. And you place your stake and you see who buys first. You can make shed loads if you bundle. Also comes in handy in the day job, if you know what I mean. Very helpful to remember the names."

"Where do they get them from?"

"Oh, who knows, maybe somebody cracked one of the ratings agencies. Maybe somebody let it leak. Disgruntled. No one knows. Who cares, really. Just keep 'em coming. Ah shit!"

Reg was looking at the board, "Enrique Maas, you got

me. That'll teach me. That chap, Tim Wilkes, he must be desperate. Maybe he's got a mortgage or something. Follow up on tomorrow."

We must have done a hundred head to heads. Reg would buy us drinks and we'd spec on when he'd get to the bar, when he'd get back. I made probably tens of thousands that night. Once it got toward morning, I started chasing this one mark, David something or other, around various different sites. I looked at his friends on FriendList. They were all suspicious. Clearly at least half were buys. Why do these idiots do it? Everyone knows they're fakes. I opened his cred scores and they were way over-valued given the fakes he had lined up. I hate to say it, but by dawn I expect the poor chap was a Contestant. I'm like that, once there's blood in the water, I can't shut it off. And these rooms will let you go. They don't turf you out at all, so you have to watch yourself. There's no natural light in the room, but if you go to the toilets there's usually a window you can open in one of the stalls. If you're wondering how far off day is, you stand on the seat and turn back the metal or the shade they have over the window, you look out and see whether the sun is up. Every time, every single time, I'm praying to see darkness.

Recap 27/6/2078

It's a full week in Ambridge, not least thanks to Adel Archer's unique approach to keeping his salmon farm that he's been renting from Oliver in a small lake they created together by Nightingale Farm. Adel's fish have sea lice and Oliver is not best pleased when he sees the latest treatment, delivered by drone from a farming conglomerate, is turning out to be a total waste of money. Adel heads into the village where he catches up with Tad and Jemima who are positively gushing as they wait for the Delivery Drone at the old post office. They can't wait to tell Adel about the new cloning and 3-D printing operation they're introducing at their farm. They're hosting the harvest fete and plan to use their printer to serve the guests rather than splashing out on hiring staff. Adel doesn't know whether to laugh or cry when they offer him a proto-type brisket.

Gerry and Fatima aren't getting on so well with the repairs to their cottage which bore the brunt of the Am's latest flood. Fatima wants Gerry to sell the house and move back into 'civilisation' in Birmingham, but Gerry can't say good-bye to the house he was born in. Good job he doesn't know Fatima has 'accidentally' listed the flat on MoveTV. Gerry might want to bone up on his specialist subject before he goes back into the cellar to clear more debris.

At Home Farm, Edward is training a new group of recruits for the picking season. It's a bit of a job getting this group up to scratch with the latest efficiency techniques. The app he's used, Maestro, allowed him to find workers for the harvest but seriously, are these former delivery drivers - made redundant when their company went driverless - and dancers whose academy was sold out from under them before they could finish their course, going to come together to be a proper gang? Edward is hopeful but despairing. His natural state...

Stay up to date with the latest from Ambridge, receive audio and recaps delivered directly to your inbox, or uploaded if you're an Isles Broadcasting Corporation neural dust user.

Abstract for consideration for Autumn 2093 Conference, Ron Sun Institute of Computational Linguistics

This paper will examine the phenomenon referred to as the "Great Flattening" from a dynamic phonological perspective. Using corpuses of data derived from hours of broadcast media and personal interviews, the researchers will consider the question of whether the so-called Great Flattening reflects fundamental changes in phono-syntactic understandings, or whether the phenomenon was merely a function of social convention. The researchers consider in detail the way the Flattening affected syntactically significant phonological boundaries, particularly with regard to epenthesis. This paper posits that apparent phono-syntactic changes may not, as is presently thought, be irreconcilable with earlier models of the interaction of phonology and syntax. The Great Flattening appears, when studied at scale to be less influential than previously thought regarding speech patterns, while it nevertheless does represent one of the largest scale reconcilings of global linguistic practice in recorded history (and likely unrecorded as well). The researchers speculate that the Flattening may be more ephemeral than is presently assumed, as, while the broad reconciliation of speech performance within and across languages has been remarkable, pockets, particularly high status pockets of urban populations do not adhere to canonical 'Flattening Conventions' and attendant lexical reductions.

Designer Neurons

ABOUT US

Designer Neurons started in the year 2074 by Duncan Heals and Martin Marquez. Duncan was a fashion journalist at the time, and he was living with Martin who was doing a medical degree at UCL in a small flat on Cecilia Street in the west London suburb of Dalston.

Duncan spent his days in the cafes and restaurants of west London, meeting and chatting to the luminaries of the global fashion world. As he met these Innovators, he always posed the same question at the end of his interviews: Where will fashion go next? As anyone who has listened to his podcast knows, each of the designers, writers, holo-models, vloggers, executives, and buyers that he spoke to had a different answer!

At the same time, Martin was in his own personal lockdown, in a rental carrel provided by a company his Uni was partnering with, devouring books on human anatomy, physiology, neuroscience, osteology, the works! Over dinner (and a bottle of Hennessy) one sultry evening in August, they found themselves talking about their respective futures, where the next decade would take them, who they wanted to be (and who they didn't want to be). While they both loved their work, each felt that there was something lacking in the career pathways they were pursuing. As the clock ticked on towards dawn and Duncan and Martin found themselves deeper into their drinks cabinet than they'd planned and wading in the deepest water of their respective professions. What was the use of fashion? How could medicine transform minds and bodies for the better? What was success? What was empathy? What was failure? What was isolation? What was life itself? The night ended with them in their back garden singing a dawn chorus. To hear Duncan tell it, they were in the middle of a banging Ghostswag remix of a Thalia Extremity track when he had a brainstorm. A remix is a kind of reinvention of a track: it's the original song, but it's also different, something totally new. What if people could be remixed? Duncan thought about his friends, hungry young designers, buyers, writers, musicians, painters, everyone he knew was dying to reinvent themselves; they just didn't know how. Martin thought about patients he'd treated during his residency. Sometimes medicine is a straightforward process: you see a broken bone, you set it, it heals. Other times, it's not so simple, sometimes a person's entire life has to change for them to optimise their health.

That night, the seed was planted for Designer Neurons. The next morning - well, more like the afternoon! - both a little worse for wear, our heroes had a late breakfast at one of the buzzy cafes on Kingsland Road. Over Daventry-grown heirloom avocado on toast, Duncan said he'd had an idea: it might sound crazy, but Martin should hear him out. He'd been reading a lot of sad stories in medical history textbooks about people in what used to be the UK, and, especially the Old US, who had been waiting for organs to be transplanted. There was nothing that could be done about the availability of organs in those days but there was a company that pointed the way to a less barbaric reality. Martin was recounting to Duncan the story of Nouriel Faraj, one of the most revered figures in Firm-Era medicine. Faraj was the founder of a company that found a way to match corporate philanthropy programmes with organ donation schemes in the Old US. In exchange for paying for the procedure, the corporation would have their logo burned into the organ that was transplanted, and participating hospitals would display a small banner over, say, their cardiac surgery theatre, saying 'Transplants brought to you by [YOUR COMPANY NAME HERE]'.

The story of Faraj was an inspiration to everyone who read it, and no medical student in London didn't imagine there was a little of Faraj in themselves when they sat down to their medical entrepreneurship exams. The age of Faraj is long gone, today, of course. Now, organ transplants are even more efficient as MedView channel shows like *Happy Organ* demonstrate. If you need a lung or a spleen today, you can be sure you're going to get one if you're prepared to go out and make it happen! But Martin took something important from Faraj's story: the idea that a big part of what it means to be a successful medical professional is to be a dreamer. Someone who looks at the world as it is and says 'why not' rather than 'why'. The inspiration Martin took from the achievements of Nouriel Faraj were a springboard to the creation of Designer Neurons. Both Duncan and Martin started knowing that they wanted to change the world, but they didn't know exactly how they'd do it. Martin continued his studies for another year, and Duncan got deep into day-speccing, and one day, he hit the jackpot. He'd been following the ups and downs of a company based in Berlin that provided insurance for spec attacks on people's credit ratings. These insurers, he thought, were notoriously Coin poor and he took a chance shorting them. The rest is history, the great spec cred unwinding of 2077 was underway, and by the end of a torrid weekend, Duncan had more capital than he knew what to do with. But of course, he did know what to do with it (hint: change the world). It just took him a while to figure out exactly how he was going to do it.

As Martin finished the last year of MedUni and his residency, Duncan used his new capital to indulge in his great passion. He returned to fashion but this time not as a lowly scribe, but as an Innovator (albeit one who hadn't quite gotten around to his first innovation). He spent a year travelling around the world, Fashion Weeks in all the great fashion Firmvilles: New York, Milan, LA, Paris, Madrid, Tangier, Tel Aviv, Toronto, São Paulo, Buenos Aires, Rotterdam, Rome, Athens, Istanbul, Sofia, İncirlik, Sarajevo, St. Petersburg, Tokyo, Shanghai, Juba, Iowa City, Dubai, Portland, Ramallah, even Modesto, soaking up all the trends and ideas he could. It was an incredible adventure and it gave him his next idea. The idea that brought you here today.

As he traveled between the cities of his tour, Duncan saw a lot of the same stars. He even became friendly with more than a few. Outside the venues, fans were gathered in their thousands to catch a glimpse, get an autograph or just absorb some of the amazing aura that such superstars exude. On the plane back to London from Dubai, Duncan started making his way through some of the papers he'd asked Martin to send him on medicine and culture. One of the most powerful pieces he read was about a project deep in the ancient days of the web called the Visible Human Project. The project involved a man named Joseph Jernigan who was a convicted murderer who was about to be put to death in the Old US. Before he was executed, Jernigan was persuaded by his spiritual counsellor to take part in the Visible Human Project, a project undertaken by a group of medical academics who wanted to build a digital map of the entire human body. To do it, they needed to have full access to human organs which they would need to dissect and scan so that a full record was available. The reasonably 'fresh' body of the executed killer would provide them with access to reasonably healthy organs to scan. Jernigan agreed to participate, and, through a series of painstaking anatomical and technological endeavours, the Visible Human Project was realised. Despite its dark and grisly origins, the project really struck a chord with Duncan. He fell asleep on the plane after reading the article, and by the time he touched down at Isle Airport Slough, Designer Neurons was effectively born. He couldn't wait to tell Martin! When Martin heard what Duncan was cooking up, he couldn't believe his ears. TBH, he wasn't completely sure how it fit into the public service mission he'd been dedicating himself to for the past few years, but he trusted Duncan and let him guide the project from its infancy to the present. Designer Neurons now has offices in New York, London, Dubai, Singapore, and Tegucigalpa.

FAQ

So what does Designer Neurons do, exactly?

The idea is simple. Using technology similar to that of the VHP but using today's far more advanced tech in cloning, imaging, and AI, DN scans the bodies of participating celebrities from the inside out. A sophisticated reference database is constructed, and researchers carefully map the structures and functions of the muscles, nerves and organs of each participating celebrity. This gives us a full understanding not only of what these stars are made of, but of what it means to actually experience being them. Anyone can put on a celebrity mask, or log into a celeb MindStream, and a few people who are rich enough can have plastic surgery to look like their favourite celebrities, but that's only skin deep. With the procedures pioneered by DN, we can show you what it's really like to BE that celebrity.

That's the basic idea, but how does it work? Well, we're happy to tell you that despite the sophistication of the technology involved, the procedure itself is fairly simple. Our clients' bodies are scanned by our in-house CAT, PET, and fMRI devices. Their entire neurological profile is uploaded to our in house Cloud where our technicians compare and contrast the client's profile with the celebrity whose neuro-profile they would like to be converted to. The whole process only takes a few hours. Think of it like an oil change, with a twist! Our lab techs then configure a series of treatments that reconcile the existing neurology of the client with that of the celebrity, at the end of our process - course length may vary depending on the proximity of age, sex, ethnicity and general health of the client and the target celebrity - you will have the exact neurological make up of your chosen celebrity. You'll never have to ask yourself again what it might feel like to be Flex Johnson, you'll know exactly what it's like!

Now for a few of the concerns many of our clients sometimes voice. In any medical procedure, there are always risks, but a well-trained medical team and lots of preliminary planning can minimise the risks so that procedures, while not entirely risk-free, pose minimal health risks for clients. Though our staff consists of highly trained medical professionals at every level, the procedure is quite invasive and it literally affects every single neuron in the body. Neurons can be quite sensitive, and, therefore, are easily damaged. Thus, at DN we use a general anaesthetic when we are doing the scan (optional) and the conversion (mandatory), but even taking every precaution, the procedure can involve nerve damage, paralysis, and in extremely limited circumstances, death. We ask that clients consider the larger context however, as with any procedure, even simple procedures like tonsil nano-bombardments or disc replacements, fatalities are possible. Happily, at the time of writing we can confirm that over the course of 45,000 procedures (and counting), DN has never lost a single client, nor has the procedure resulted in any recorded incidents of long-term paralysis, blindness, impotence, incontinence, exogenous neuropathies, or other major illnesses.

Now that questions of safety are out of the way, let's talk about the fun stuff, *what will it be like?*

Will I Have the Thoughts of My Celebrity? This is a tough question. On one level, we have to tell you the answer is probably not. The thoughts you have will be your own, but that's not to say that you won't have some of the same thoughts as your celebrity. For instance, if you're eating the same food as the celebrity you become, you're very likely to experience the same thoughts as you experience what will be the same sensations. This is almost certainly going to be true of sexual experiences as well, particularly holo-sex with digitally generated celebrities. Our philosophy at DN is that you're getting the best of both worlds. You get to know what it feels like for your favourite celeb when she's dining out and/or having sex, and you know that you know what it's like for her. That's pretty much the definition of win-win in our book! Think of it this way: you're having your thoughts (software) with the thinking matter (hardware) of your celebrity.

Will I Still Be Me? Of course you'll still be you, that's the one thing no one has ever managed to change - and no one probably never will! You'll still retain your full range of conscious thoughts, memories, and basic personality traits, you will, however, have the sensory experiences, sensitivities and neuro-motor responses of the celebrity you select. Think of it as being in the driver's seat in a car that handles like Denzel tha Prince.

Will My Friends and Family Recognise Me? Of course they will, unless, of course you opt for plastic surgery, too (please see our rates on our Prep Services page for details). It is up to individual clients of DN to disclose the procedure to friends and family. From the outside, you'll look exactly the same, but you'll feel - in more ways than one - totally differently. DN promises full confidentiality and fully complies with the legal requirements for personal and medical data in all the Firm territories where it operates.

Is the Process Reversible? At present, given the intensive character of the procedure, it is not possible to reverse it without risk of serious nerve damage. This does not mean that that reversal will never be possible, it just means that for the foreseeable future, DN is not planning to offer reversion procedures. Once you decide which celebrity you want to be, you're going to be that person for a while, so, as they say, choose, but choose wisely.

If you have other questions, feel free to drop us an email at info@designerneurons.tv. We look forward to hearing from you!

For Immediate Release

Karyn Hormel Gallery is proud to present the new exhibition of works by Nadya Surface. Surface's new work, 'CloudStead', will be produced over the course of the exhibition and will explore the ways in which value creation and the mechanics of production are realised in a trans-planetary economy. Surface has worked with the meteorological and business departments of various campuses of LongRiver Education Service Universities in locations around the world to produce novel nephological structures (clouds) that collectors can scan and reproduce in physical form should they so choose. During the opening, orders will be taken from collectors within the Hormel Gallery space in Marlow, as well as from around the world. Surface will produce the clouds at the time and location requested in the various cities in which partner-universities are located.

Nadya Surface is renowned for works that interrogate the assumptions that underpin contemporary social, politicraftly, and economic relations. Her work challenges the most sacred shibboleths of Neo-Firmatarianism and poses pressing and urgent questions about human agency, care, and interplanetary extractive endeavours. Previous works include 'Subtle Theft Auto' in which Surface recorded the time lag between her car 'thefts' of various parked vehicles in Paris and the issuance to her telephone of ownership transfer fees as determined by local drone monitors.

**Nadya Surface, Karyn Hormel Gallery, its directors, and all associated Firms and trusts, as well as LongRiver Education Services University and all associated entities, Firms and trusts, accept no responsibility for adverse weather conditions, disruptions, or modelling errors (financial, meteorological, social, or otherwise) 'CloudStead' works may cause.*

Data-Self Partnered

Oh, I'd heard about it happening, but I always thought that it was some kind of hoax. Everyone had one, that you just kind of had to assume given how much data they actually have for you, but no one I knew had ever actually met theirs yet, their shadow. We knew they were there, of course, information moulded into a sharper focus outline of us. We knew these shadows had helped to shape us, intimately but from a fundamental remove. You might think of them as setting a table at which we could dine, the decor and menu selected by knowledge greater and more deliberate than anything we could achieve ourselves by simple introspection. We could sit, and we could choose, or try to, from the dishes they had set out for us. We could imaginate every comfort and see it before us, the only thing we weren't allowed to do was to relax.

Our shadows were present in jokes, mostly. Our fears rendered inert by our awareness of our own fear. That these beings were more real than we were, that they knew things about us that we didn't. Humour was more of a shield than a sword, a way to convince ourselves that there was no risk, not really, of the shadows creating problems for us. They were distant family members to be recalled on certain occasions, but never sought out casually. They were an abstraction. They were immaterial. They could even be fun. There would be stories on April Fool's Day for example, everyone would laugh: a data clone was chosen as the director of some minor Firm. A data clone sports league was being created by an eccentric trillionaire living on an island in an Exception Zone. The first story like this I remembered reading turned out to be true. It was about a woman who had gone to court in the

St. Lawrence Firmzone to be allowed to marry her data shadow. It sounded like one of those old privacy campaign stunts we'd heard about from the early years of the century. Some activists would find some absurdity in the laws and push it to what they thought was a humorous extreme, counting on the good sense of society to prevail, but as the courts changed after the Fall of the States, they couldn't assume a benign social gaze would greet these kinds of hijinks. The humour of suing your younger self for libel, or similar, drained away.

The story about the data marriage had a lot of interesting strands. The woman who did it was an adjunct professor at a prestigious Uni near Toronto, Ewan Cameron College. She had apparently found her data through brokers, or through lawsuits or something, and what she'd found suggested that the person that the web thought she was was much wealthier and successful than who she actually was. So she worked with some people from her university's computer science lab to create a holo-bot to embody and perform her shadow so that she could converse directly with it. The lab had her recovered data to work with, and she gave them some specifics for the kind of personality she wanted her shadow to have. The shadow could advise her, she told the Idea Press, to make better life decisions. In the end, she decided that if she married her data shadow, she would have better life chances than marrying a physical person. Announcing her plan on social media got her lots of writing gigs, far more than she'd had before writing about her obscure, subjacent academic interest, something to do with language processing or phonology maybe. A publisher offered her a book deal, her first. I wonder if her data shadow advised her to do the whole thing now that I think back on it. It was quite a shrewd plan. Ultimately, though, she lost. But the judge who rejected her petition to marry her shadow did so on very narrow grounds. He wrote that it wasn't clear that the data shadow simulation could actually respond in the same way a person could to a marriage proposal, and, therefore, that rendered any contract undertaken with a data shadow void on the grounds that it could not be proven to not be coerced. Clearly it was a decision aimed at trying to stop people doing financial deals with holo-bots and shadows, but the headlines and think pieces were all about the marriage side of it. The woman lodged an appeal of some kind; over time I stopped paying attention to the case, but the idea clearly caught on. One day coming back from the office, I noticed in the Boxpark on Berkeley Square that there's now a shop that can arrange dates with other people's digital shadows. Marriage wasn't allowed, of course, but no one could stop these simul-dates.

Think pieces really started flowing about the topic once other companies got into the act. Pretty soon, there were more shadow dating apps than real ones. 'Data self care' became an expression you'd see on various posts. Columnists argued that the arrangement might actually lead people to better lives, and indirectly help others improve their off-line situations. This is from an article titled 'A Caress from the Invisible Hand? Count Me In!'. It's only one, but there were dozens like it:

> *...And who's to say it's any less real than normal dating? In fact, data dating services might be quite a bit more honest than the old fashioned way. Ladies, how many times haven't you found the 'Pro-Self' you meet on a date is quite a different creature to the bloke you come back to three months later when he's speccing in his pants on the sofa and listening to IceTrap at all hours? Sure it might take some getting used to, you're not going to be holding hands with Data DreamBoat while you walk to the village market on the weekend, but look on the bright side; sure, today you may be stuck at home working while the partner of your dreams is falling for Data You, and that might seem a little bit unfair, but the more interest your data self gets, the more likely advertisers - and, crucially, employers - are to notice. You might be getting a leg up without leaving your sofa. And, the more popular Data You becomes, the more confident you should feel. Take a chance, swipe right to swipe up the social ladder. You might just find someone. Maybe even the person dating your shadow!*

People took the advice. It wasn't common, but maybe once a week you'd see a person-shadow couple out in the park or at a bar together. Some people took it to the next level and 3-D printed parts of the shadows so that they could hold hands. At least. I had a certain morbid curiosity about shadow dating, I should say, but I never actually followed up. I don't know if I'd have been able to take the process seriously, or if I could take myself seriously if I did. It was all too close to the world of sexgrams and love-gigging that were spreading everywhere. It was amazing that everything, everything could be catered to now, and priced, the right angle for a photograph, the right script for a phone call, and, of course, the right act when or if the Special Moment came. Everything had premium subscriptions and VIP tiers. It was overwhelming, and if anything, more panic inducing than dating was when I was younger. I was working a lot, too, though, beyond the usual progress-working, my flat had just come up on *Movers & Shakers*, and I had to make the case for why I should be allowed to stay there - and to have some spare Creds on hand in case I got forced out. Shadows interested me, but the thought of them having an interest in me was something I was even less prepared for than my *M&S* appearance.

The day it happened, when I heard the bell, I thought it was just my friend Eric who had been coaching me through the process. He'd successfully won his *M&S* spot a couple of months back - and fended off a challenge from someone who claimed to own the freehold after they saw him during the previous appearance. I was picking his brain now on a weekly basis for information and gaming strategies. I opened the door expecting to see Eric, and suddenly I was looking into my own eyes.

I couldn't speak. Initially I thought it might be some kind of mind game from my opponents on *Movers & Shakers*, trying to rattle me so I'd screw up and they'd get my flat. But no, it was just me, or my shadow, that is. He nodded to me briskly. I nodded back very slowly. He motioned with his hand, or my hand, I suppose, our hand to be let in. I instinctively stood back, and felt a surge of regret pass through every cell in my body.

'I take it you weren't expecting me.'

'Yes.'

'Yes you weren't expecting me, or yes you were?'

'The former.'

'I can see you're not going to be easy to work with.'

My shadow informed me that he was part of a new project my bank was launching. The increasing interest in shadows meant that they had no choice but to become more active in the world. It was unfair to them, and to us, their life-partners - as my shadow referred to me - that we only experienced them by implication. The bank was launching a pilot programme for 'risky customers', which I learned I was. We would be given free visits for a year from our data shadows to help us to make better financial decisions.

'That's very generous. I just don't feel like I want this service right now, maybe in a year, or after I finish with *Movers*--'

'The "service", as you call me, is not optional, but I am free. Charges will only be applied if you insist on discontinuing the service, however, and, as someone with your best interests at heart, I would advise you not to do that. Simply put, you can't afford not to speak to me. I mean that in more ways than one.'

My data shadow understood that there would be a peri od of adjustment, but I had to see things from his - our - point of view.

'I live in a very competitive environment. I can't risk your decision-making holding me back from what I'm capable of.'

The visits would be regular. Once per Seven Day. I asked if I could select the time of the appointments.

'Unfortunately, we can't allow that. The saccade scanner our employer has installed on your computer will tell me when you're home, and when an opportune moment to appear arises. You can appeal, of course, but, again, the process can be quite daunting. I'll have a brochure sent along tomorrow with the finer points. For the moment, I think we should simply touch on a few general themes this evening. We'll be covering them in greater depth as we go forward.'

We only spoke for about half an hour, mostly about insurance, 'It's the kind of thing that can keep you from ending up on *Movers & Shakers* in the first place,' and good vs. bad debt, 'Have you considered setting up a personalised account to sell your debt to speccers? There are facilities that my employer can offer you to cover a range of options, you can even buy it yourself if you like'.

I can't say it wasn't enlightening, but I can't say I enjoyed it either. When it was time for him to go, I didn't know what to say, so I just said, 'I'll see you - or me? - later?'

My shadow turned and waved before he disappeared, 'Terence, just say "we". You'll want to get used to it.'

Blood Work

The plague came. We'd had warnings, historical precedents, but when it came, no one was really prepared. We repeated all the same mistakes, lived through all the same past scenarios again. When it finally burned itself out, two point five million deaths globally, everyone seemed to collectively exhale, but no one fully understood why it had stopped. There were vaccines, but they moved into the market place much more slowly than the virus. There wasn't even time for a good MedShow to emerge about it. Channels that used to run MedShows non-stop suddenly became home shopping channels or revivalist channels. The doctors and the researchers had mapped the virus fairly quickly, by historical standards, but getting drugs to market took a long time, and there were Firm Rule issues, like who could distribute competitors' vaccines in different management zones. The problem never really got resolved, I don't even know if it can be resolved, you'd have to rewire society completely if you wanted people to surrender patents or allow competitors into markets for humanitarian reasons alone. People changed afterward. Maybe a new suspicion of the way Firms did things started creeping in. To a lot of people this wasn't the kind of 'competition in action' they'd been told to live by. If competition was the ideal state of life, why, when it counted did the Firms prevent it in their own back gardens?

People changed, usually in low key personal ways, but there were general trends too. For example, the appetite for risk everyone prized so highly, it wasn't gone exactly, but people were different for quite a while afterward. You'd talk to people and they'd talk about the pre-Firm period, almost nostalgically, 'those were simpler times', 'people looked out for each other more'. There was a sense that those were more certain and secure times. University types would talk about bringing back 'governments' maybe on a trial basis, just in emergencies, but it was a fad, once things started to return to a kind of normality, these kinds of thoughts drifted out of Idea Press headlines and message boards until only some half-crazy dons wanting attention for their teaching channels ever talked about it. The plague did genuinely stun the Firms, though, you could see that. There were a lot of panic hires, applied genetics, biodiversity consultants. Out of nowhere people were getting Coin level jobs when they should have still been earning creds or burning off debt. Everybody you knew, everybody's half-employed cousin, every teenager working in a cafe was going to go to uni and go into LifeMed. It was a fad, too, once the Firms realised their new generation of experts weren't telling them much, wages went down and everyone went back to their previous lifelong dreams, but that gold rush did some good too. It did me some good at least.

BloodBuddy was the big new firm to rise out of the ashes the plague left behind. They didn't have a plague treatment, or a vaccine, but they hit on the idea of how to sell certainty about health, or, if not certainty, then answers, and answers are as good as certainty for a lot of people. BloodBuddy developed a test kit you could take in your home. You bled into a little vial and then some little transistor whirrs for about ten minutes and it gives you a 'blesstimate' of how long you can expect to live. Again, it's a scary idea. There are some answers you don't know that you don't want to know. It took a while for people to adopt it, but it became addictive, the idea that you could actually see the boundary of your own life in clear digital letters on a screen. That first generation of the app got people interested, but it wasn't very profitable. The problem with answers - even bad answers - is they're an ending point, a kind of last word. Business needs the conversation to keep going. The longer the better. BloodBuddy decided to become a subscriber service. Blesstimates now came in three tiers: Free, which was just the raw score, then Premium which told you how long you could expect to live if you followed a set of prescribed exercise programmes and subscribed to the monthly panel of treatments and supplements of BloodBuddy's corporate partners. These were all based on a data sharing agreement you signed with BloodBuddy at the beginning of a Premium subscription. Then there was the Platinum, which offered you all of the other tiers' services but also included access to personal digital trainers who would smilingly guide you through the regimes and monitor your progress. You could chat to the trainers at any time, about any subject really - which was a good research basis for BloodBuddy's new mental health service which they introduced five years after the tier system. After a decade, Bloodbuddy was the biggest healthcare company in Firm Zone Isles. They really grew when they brought in a spin-off for younger people they partnered with schools to provide. They called it Little Bleeders. Every year they aimed to test 5 million more children to estimate and enhance life outcomes. The idea was that if you knew exactly how to change your life, even if you didn't always stick to it, you could be better off. Maybe, you could even beat the odds.

But the odds have their own logic.

When things got complicated for BloodBuddy was because a regional interfirm council got involved. The people on these councils aren't business people. They're a holdover, a compromise with the past. The locals appoint them, but they're all subject to Firm approval - though firms don't usually bother vetting them until there's already a problem. In practice, they act more like consultants than anything else, no one knows what councillors really do. They come to conferences, eat the free food and wine, get their pictures taken with Firm bosses and sneak off to leave. Most of the time they do nothing, but sometimes they can do good work, balancing the interests of firms so that there aren't inter-firm conflicts that end up costing lives. BloodBuddy had negotiated with one of these councils to do a regional advertising partnership and cred-saving scheme. The idea was if you met certain health and fitness goals, your annual firm dues could be refunded to a certain percentage. It certainly seemed like a win-win. People loved it, and it fostered competition, but a competition with no losers which was something people were hungry for at that time. The campaign made headlines all across the Isles when a 100-year-old man from Surbiton bet his neighbours that he'd beat his predicted lifespan by exercising more and giving up his daily bottle of gin. It was all quite compelling. Idea Press carried stories on him most days. The months went by as the countdown to Barry The Force (as the Press started calling him)'s appointed hour. When the day arrived, the cameras were flashing in Barry The Force's Surbiton garden, snapping him, very much alive and enjoying an early afternoon G&T. He collected the bet money from his neighbours, and donated it to a Contestant Class Brain Games training programme. At the time of writing, Barry The Force is still drinking his G&Ts and enjoying watching the afternoon quiz shows, all the while waiting for one of his donor children to turn up on The Prodigies. The story of Barry The Force sparked a lot of discussion about speccing and health. People wondered if, since it was ok for Barry The Force to bet on his health, might it maybe be ok to bet on other people's health outcomes, too? And not just in office whip-rounds, proper speccing.

Leprechaun Spreads was the first firm to take the plunge. It was PR at first, a kind of flutter of their own: they said they'd match any fitness or longevity challenges taken up in the most deprived wards in Lower Britannia Firm Zone for the next six months. People took to the offer like hotcakes to the point where they had to stop the programme after three months because their own probability models started looking scary. They shouldn't have worried. By six months in, they'd made billions of Coins, but Leprechaun did the smart thing and touted the success stories, the fairly rare instances when someone beat the BloodBuddy health models the company was using to determine bets. It looked like easy money, if you didn't look too carefully. A glance at the local Idea Press and it looked like all of Walsall was beating what Bloodbuddy had predicted for them. No one knew about the exercise heart attacks, and the crash diet casualties. They just saw a healthier Isles just on the other side of an afternoon's low effort speccing.

Offices doing an annual office health flutter became a regular thing. The Press made sure the good news was always there to ensure a crop of new contestants. The scale led to the first dark pools getting established, and that's how the real problems started. Some mutual funds did the maths when they saw Leprechaun Spreads' quarterly reports and realised a whole new world was waiting for them. Taking a short position on health challenges was where you could really cash in. But when you pour in money at that scale, you want to secure your investment. That's how I ended up in this job.

I was a Contestant for a long time, but it got so boring. I didn't like sitting for hours in endless green rooms, poised on miserable little plastic chairs watching as the numbers flashed up on the display. When yours came, you'd walk to the window to see what show you were being offered. If it wasn't anything you wanted, you went straight back to the end of the queue. It's a kind of life you can get used to, but it's nothing you should settle for. That last day, I saw my number come up and I walked to where the teller hologram was projected on the window and she said,

'Congratulations, Natalie, you've been selected for *Cowpunchers Anonymous*!'

The form printed, and as I listened to the printer carriage screeching all the letters into place, I asked myself if I could really take six months training to be a rodeo clown and stand up comic for the show. I pictured myself in the stupid make up in a rodeo ring with a wild bull in a pen just a few feet away. I looked at the form. The hologram blinked its eyes. I looked back at the queue and I just turned and walked down the endless rows of seats. Someone was already walking past me to pick up the *Cowpunchers Anonymous* slot. He looked very eager.

It was for the best, at least I'd say it was a better choice given what was on offer. I talked to some people on the fringe of the health data business and they gave me a few leads for what the Investment firms call 'supplemental services' in their Firm Due Filings. I found a role very quickly. And I like it. I'm my own boss, but obviously, there are stereotypes. To start, no one likes to call themselves a hitman. It's tawdry. It's tainted. It's gendered, too. But most of all, it's inaccurate. To say I'm a freelance hitman suggests that I kill people. That's not what I do. It's not how I see it at least. Most of my job is just strategy. A Firm comes to me, say they sell snacks, I find them ways of cracking into people's feeds, make sure they know that Creamy's is still in business, and their fudge cream pies are still as delicious as ever. You can make a living from scale cracks, video games, for example, are full of holes, and all you need to do is stay one step ahead of their mods, stick an advert here or there in the background of some scene and you're guaranteed to dent BloodBuddy models. Snack firms aren't exactly sure how much we're worth, but they pay. If you want a little more certainty, there's that word again, you can take targeted jobs. Those are harder, but they're far more rewarding. You have to be thinking constantly, how can I keep this slob from getting to the gym? How can I get some pizza into her gob? Usually it's just innocent stuff, somebody in a Cred firm betting against somebody else making the office's weekly whip round goals. Sometimes though, it can be serious. You have to make your own decisions on those cases. I never take anyone under fifty. I stick to men. I feel like the numbers are on my side there, numbers and history. And I always make sure there are other explanations for what happens to them. The world is a mess after all, but if you know what you're doing, often uncertainty can be the best friend you have.

Banged Up in Barra

The Firms would have you believe they've completely abolished the nation-state era prison industrial complex. Take this statement on Firm Responsibility from Edelweiss Investments, who govern the territories that used to be known as the upper midwest of the Old United States. It's characteristic of the way Firms like to present themselves:

> *In 2055, when Edelweiss formally assumed management of the territory between the Missouri River and the Allegheny River north of the Blue Ridge Mountains, we put an end to the vast system of exploitation and repression instigated by unaccountable state-based enforcement bodies including more than five hundred and fifty individual police departments, all of whom were running inadequate and inhumane carceral facilities in the territories. Now, local populations, particularly those most affected by police-based violence and brutality can go about their business without worrying about unjust harassment, or worse.*

Sounds pretty nifty, eh? But what if I told you there were hundreds of Firm-run penal colonies throughout the territory of the Old US?

What's that you say? 'Old habits die hard'? 'Only in Old America'? Well, what if I told you that the Isles also have Firm-run penal colonies that are equally opaque? I'm Paul Rhodes, and I've come to the Isle of Barra to investigate one such facility and take you, Behind Bars.

I came to the Isle of Barra on a Super(ca)b ferry. No ferry firms service Barra since 2062. All traffic in and out is done by Firm-servicing Firms, but good old Super(ca)b will go anywhere where Coins are accepted.

I expected to find a facility shrouded in secrecy and security, to have to blag my way in, or use the skills I developed as a member of the Special Security Services doing Firm-stability work in the Pacific Sector, but to my surprise my Super(ca)b was greeted on the shore by an employee of the Prison. Looks like they were expecting me. They told me that a drone had picked up my Super(ca)b near Liverpool and tracked me the rest of the way. One can't be too careful in a place like this, they told me. I guess not. I'm sure the lags feel the same way, right?

'We don't like to call them "prisons"; that evokes distasteful historical practices that we proudly define our rehabilitation project against.'

The Firm who run this prison, Frei and Einfach, is based in Munich, but they were hired by the Firms that manage the Isles to import best practices in modern imprisonment for Isle-based offenders. As drones hovered overhead - none were armed, none that I could see at least - we made our way through the open air facility. Prisoners were working, some were in a ring of dirt fighting. I asked my handler what was going on, were staff just allowing a prison fight to happen in broad daylight?

'The prisoners are live-streaming the event. It's a pay per view. We encourage entrepreneurial endeavours on the part of our co-workers.'

'You call the prisoners "co-workers"?'

'We believe it fosters a sense of common purpose and destigmatises those in our care. I do wish you'd stop using the word "prisoner" to refer to them. That is a term we have outgrown.'

Reinhard, the bloke in charge, was smooth but I knew there was more to the story. If you want to find out what it's like *Behind Bars in Barra*, the full documentary is available on my Vid-E.O. page, OnTheRhodes. Subscribers can also join a weekly chat about Isle prison conditions and anything else that happens to be on my mind every Fifth Day afternoon.

Hope to see you there. In the meantime, look after yourself, eh, mate.

Corporate Unrest

After a certain point, it no longer made sense to distance the company from the violence. The first news reports had been terrifying for the marketing teams. Gang fights all over London. A 15-year-old stabbed, in intensive care. Two days later, dead. The only motive, apparently, was that he was wearing clothes with the wrong label. No one in the offices understood. The team deployed to do damage control called up the mother firm in Los Angeles. Oh, yes. They were familiar. They'd been through it before. In fact it was a sad chapter of company lore. They patched the London team's leader, Obafemi, through to the company historian in Burbank.

'Yes, it was a local phenomenon so there's plenty of archival material here.'

'It went on for years?'

'Decades.'

'Decades? How? Wasn't anyone....how did you stay in business?'

'It was a different time. They didn't know how to manage inequality then. It was all very mixed up. I don't suppose you know about the Intifada that followed either?'

'I don't think so no.'

'It was in the 1990s. Lots of young people, Black for the most part, had been harassed for years by the nation-state shock troops. You've heard of "police", right?'

'Yeah, definitely. They're like the IP Enforcers or something, no?'

'Not exactly, but that's not the worst analogy. Anyway, they used to harass and rob and beat on these young Black men for years, then there was a guy, Rodney King, they filmed the beating—'

'The police filmed it?'

'No, just a person. It went around the channels. There was a trial, they let the police officers walk with no serious charges. Grim stuff. Very grim. Anyway, there was an Intifada afterward. Black people, other demographics, all out on the streets. It's ironic, they took it all out on shops and stores, companies! The exact wrong targets - the only ones who could help them! - but Fog of War, and of course, the police were armed and dangerous back then.'

'Terrible.'

'Very.'

'So what happened?'

'What do you mean?'

'What happened to stop it all?'

'Well, nothing, really. It just burnt itself out. Fights started up between different groups again, politicians made promises that everyone forgot about, and then, not so long afterward, mid-twenty first century, they went back to stuff you're seeing over there, the Brand Wars. That lasted a long time. Forty years. All very low-level and ring-fenced off from mainstream life, but still.'

'But, I mean, what do we do, then? Now, I mean.'

The company historian was silent for a few seconds. Obafemi heard him exhale deeply through the line, then he gave a sort of muffled laugh.

'Ride it out. It will pass.'

'And you say none of these brands in the wars went out of business?'

'None. Well some did, but not for that reason. Just the usual market judgments.' 'Huh.'

'Yeah, it's a head-scratcher.'

'So you think we should….'

"Ride it out."

The London team was very disturbed when Obafemi brought back the advice from HQ. 'Ride it out?' That could take years!

And these Brand Wars, that was the 90s. Did HQ have any idea how much faster markets moved now? Had they never heard of social media? Had they been living under a rock? The 1990s? Those were the old Gen Xers they'd read about. The ones who had never done anything about anything. Slackers was the term that came down the decades to sum them up. Apparently they'd embraced it for themselves. The Gen Xers were a cautionary tale about social decadence in most Advanced Placement History modules for Uni now. Pure nation-state mindset. The world was very different now, mind-meld media, posting armies, thought-crop teams. This wasn't the passive culture of the pre-Firm age. There were thousands of ways brand violence could get out of hand now; waiting for it to 'burn itself out' wasn't an option. Maybe that was the way the LA team would do it, living in the Old US with their Zenifornian philosophy, but things were different in London. Different histories. Even now, there were regional variations on the way Firms managed populations. Geography was still a barrier to full rationalisation, Obafemi thought. Outdated philosophies can still be protected by rivers and mountains. No, the London office was not going to let it 'burn itself out' and take hundreds of people along with it, this strange fire they found themselves surrounded by. It was up to the marketing team, they had to try to stop it.

Obafemi had led the marketing team for three years now. He'd overseen some great, even historic campaigns. The Astro-Vapour's: 'The Stars Are Shining in Your Mind'. The Nimbus Security Project campaign, 'Safe as a Cloud in the Sky', and the one he was most proud of, the No Cow vegan steak printing campaign 'No Cow, All Cow', that he estimated was responsible for a 3% reduction in overall bovine carbon emissions globally. He was on his way to Innovator status. He could feel it. Things were looking up for him at home, too. He'd just managed to move his family into inner London, a nice place in Tottenham. The idea that violence would be associated with the brand that had hired him to take them to the next level, it was beyond anything he'd learned at uni, where it was all about strategy and tactics. Brand alliances, new cog formats where you place adverts. He knew this would define his legacy at the company. He couldn't fail, and he wouldn't. That night after the call with the LA branch, he drew up a strategy. The team would partner with youth organisations in London that worked to stop crime. They'd work the channels with Celeb Contestants so that they'd have the authenticity factor. They'd donate money, maybe even his longed for bonus, and things would be brought under control. He sent the outline to his deputy, Anjali, for troubleshooting and she texted back immediately.

'Nice but obsolete.'

'?'

'Haven't you seen the newsfeeds?'

Obamfemi picked up his phone. While he was writing the strategy there was news of a second stabbing. There had already been unrest in the area, people out on the streets. Everybody knew the council in Havering was cracking down, too, they were proper reactionaries. They could expect a drone deployment if things got out of hand. Obafemi closed his eyes and rubbed his palms over his face. It was only 22.00. He could see messages cascading on his wall display. All capital letters. The regional director, Aaron, was already in holographic form in the corner of his work glasses mouthing the words 'call me now'. Obafemi pinged Anjali again, 'Do you have any ideas? ANY?'

'I might have one,' she wrote.

Obafemi managed to get Aaron's blood pressure down by saying he was already in an emergency meeting with the entire department now. The promise of having something in an hour was made, Obafemi felt not entirely by an act of his will. Anjali was waiting on another channel. She'd been watching the whole thing. Obafemi switched her mic on:

'I need your idea. Now.'

'Ok, but content warning, you're not going to like this.' Obafemi didn't like it, but the logic was undeniable. They were locked into this newscycle whether they liked it or not. They could play defence and get slaughtered, or they could go on the offensive. They would blame it all on the other brand. They had to be subtle about it, or as subtle as possible without being subtle at all. There really was no other choice; the stabbings were going to continue, but maybe if they could tag their competition with the blame, they could minimise the damage at home, and perhaps even gain some marketshare, but this wasn't the kind of thing you could say out loud, not even to yourself. It was ugly, but war is ugly, even when it's not your war.

*

They found some hungry influencers on vlogs. They told them that they had a mission for any and all aspiring hype-beasts. They told them that they were offering them a mission that the brand would be forever grateful to them for, but that they couldn't be directly associated with the campaign. I.e. the brand couldn't pay them.

They all got back with the same reply:

'Pay us? Why would you be paying us?'

All they wanted was swag. So it was arranged that there was a particular skip in Spitalfields that the influencers could go to, tucked away off Gun Street near the remains of The City. They could pick up swag there one day a week. It was random, but anyone who took part could work out a time for a pick up with a friendly bartender on Curtain Road who was interning at the brand.

It looked promising. The influencers were grinding hard, posting constantly, @ing the other brand involved night and day telling them to explain themselves. Demanding that they prove they weren't behind the campaign of violence as drones were now buzzing around demonstrations on the streets of Havering and Romford. One morning, there was a press conference, the CEO of their 'rival' was stepping down. The influencers celebrated and taunted the new CEO, 'What are you going to do? Are you serious about stopping the violence? FIGHT FIRE WITH FIRINGS!' Corks were popping in the corner office as all this was happening. Phase Two of Anjali's strategy was under way: free promo samples to the affected communities.

'It is our hope,' Obafemi wrote on the company's landing screen, 'that by making our clothes ubiquitous, we can write over the meanings others have tried to establish for us.'
The clothes, mostly workwear boiler suits that hadn't tested well in the Balkan market, disappeared quickly. The next time Obafemi saw one it was on another stabbing victim.

*

Obafemi hadn't been to bed properly for weeks. His partner had to move into a Hovershare above the canal on the outskirts of the city in Maida Vale to sleep. He sat in his living room with a bottle of NorthRegion whisky, slowly lowering its volume beneath the label's plimsoll line, watching the newsfeeds. More stabbings came, but they were already built into Anjali's model. It would be another few weeks before they were expected to taper off. Obafemi watched masses of people moving down the streets of Havering, placards aloft, FIRMS DON'T LOVE US! FIRMS NOT FAIR! HAND IN HAND, NOT BRAND VS BRAND! You could see drones floating overhead, some of the placard people would try to smack at them and would get covered in pepper paint and go down to the ground. The procession moved along and the drones filming zeroed in on what looked like a skirmish in the middle of the protest. Dozens of people were throwing punches. They all wore jackets by Obafemi's brand. He watched the first drones fire nets on the crowd but this caused more chaos than before. Some people appeared in the rival brand's gear. Someone shot down a pepper paint drone and you could see smoke nearby from a fire someone had started. Obafemi knew what was next. The smoke was there to block the drones' visual systems. The psychos on the Havering council hadn't been returning calls for a week to the Firms that administered the area demanding deescalation. The council hinted they'd use lethal drones if their control was threatened, but no one took it seriously. It was all, surely, a rhetorical pitch to frighten people back inside. Surely.

Obafemi saw them the unmistakable shape of armed drones' shadows creeping along the buildings of the high streets. Rockets tucked along their wings like deadly fruit. He turned off the newsfeed. He knew what was coming. He looked at his phone. Messages had piled up. On top was Anjali.

'Good news.'

He called her channel up.

'We just got the quarterlies in. Marketshare is through the roof.'

'There's a war on, for Scripture's sake! They've just sent out a fleet of Reapers in Havering.'

'Have they?'

Anjali went quiet and turned on the news. Fires were everywhere now. Fire drones were dropping water on buildings and people. There were strike craters.

'Oh, yes. It does look that way doesn't it?'

Aaron was breaking in on another channel. He asked Obafemi if he'd seen the coverage, seen the bodies? Seen the bodies in OUR clothes? He told Obafemi his services wouldn't be required anymore. Obafemi said nothing. He turned off Aaron's channel and was about to click Anjali off when he saw Aaron's face appear behind her in one of her home screens.

In her first press conference as the head of marketing, Anjali decried the drone strikes in Havering and said that it was time for a responsible Firm to regain control of Havering. This was what happened, she said, when you let politics back into management. A young man was standing beside her at the press conference. It was the bartender from Shoreditch. He was kitted out in an outfit Obafemi didn't recognise from any recent collections. Anjali introduced him, Bertie McDonagh, and announced that he was the regional branch services manager in the brand's militia. They would be deployed to Havering today to restore effective management. If people wanted to join the effort, for a small subscription fee, they could receive discounts on all new products for the duration of any kinetic brand-based operations. They could visit the website for more information.

CryptoProphet1

The religions never died. They were supposed to, but they were used to fighting for their place. We could waste time talking about the great minds, the professors and pundits who all told us how things were going to go now that the state had withered, at last. Some were followers of the prophet Marx, but not really very many. Most were elated about the miracle of the market finally being unleashed, some kind of truth was going to shine through at last and radiate through us like stigmata in an old painting - if you'll forgive an analogy. Among these latter, there were two major strains of thought. First, there were the Bright Ones, I think they even called their little coterie that. The ones who believed that the rise of the Firms was a step toward a kind of ideal they'd always longed for. You could find Bright Ones on both sides of what used to be called 'politics'. They're the ones who would say things like:

'Look, it's not perfect, not by any means, but it's a step toward rationality, and a materialist view of the world. That alone is a net positive. Besides, maybe we can hold off the worst of any extremism.'

Not least, you might add, by finding estimable places for ourselves in the new arrangement.

The others, I guess they'd be the 'Dim Ones' - though they didn't call themselves that - had a simpler outlook, but maybe they had a clearer view of things. They would be the ones to say things like:

'The new arrangement will allow people to be honest with themselves. That's going to be Hell, but you can have a good time in Hell once in a while.'

As it turns, out, from what we've seen recently, the operative word in that sentence is probably 'once', and the 'while' was coming to last much longer than anyone expected, and, for a lot of us, this Saturday-night-in-Hell stuff still felt like Hell These debates all became academic after a few years of conflict; all of it sparked by an ill-advised drone strike on street marches in Havering. There were the usual immolations, the kinds of terror attacks people had come to associate with religions, ironically enough. The Bright Ones, especially, took these as a kind of vindication. Soon, we'd all see. The young would save us, appalled as they'd surely be by these acts of darkness and fanaticism. The young didn't save us - spoiler alert. I'm not sure what them saving us would even have looked like. Kids with weird haircuts swapping holo-memes with each other then shooting you in the head if you were found with a rosary? Count me among the lost, though the Old Believers would count me as lost, too.

It takes a long time to come full circle, it seems. When the final ceremony had taken place, the last state surrendering to the Eur-African Firms, everyone had thought that would be the end for the Old Ways, nations, faiths, extremisms. Incidentally, a lot of historians say Eswatini had been the last state to surrender, but it wasn't. There's always a lesson to be taken from mistakes historians choose to make. Eswatini held on for a long time, and their King got a very, very good deal from the Firms in the region - that's how that entire swathe of Firmland got named Mswatia on maps. Where the mistake comes in, Eswatini was the last state that had an officially recognised national *territory* to surrender, but the last sovereign entity to go, actually, was a pseudo-state in Europe called SMOM, The Sovereign Military Order of Malta. As in the Knights of Malta, as in The Crusades from the Ancient Age. That should have been a clue as to how things might play out. The SMOMers were mostly a business by then anyway, so it made sense for them simply to reconsolidate as a Firm. I trust everyone reading has heard of MOMSTrade. That's them. The employees who move on from them - there aren't many, they offer great benefits - all talk about a weird team building exercise they have to do when they're hired where they all lay on the floor of the Head Office in groups of six in a particular pattern and then recite some text. It's mostly nonsense, but it appears to be based on a profession of faith used by the Knights Hospitallers from the times of the Crusades. Again, nobody seemed to notice that bit, but it was there to be seen.

The Firms, for their part, did their best to find a solution to the religion problem, but they hadn't really planned for what came when the nation-states started falling. This was in part because of the way the collapse happened, so randomly, and so differently in different places. In some cases it was the climate, in others economic problems and unemployment; in others it just seemed to happen because it was happening everywhere else. Once it was clear this was the way things were going everywhere, the Firms became the natural heirs of power. It only made sense. They already had people living in most of the old 'countries'. They had property, security forces, and a clear internal hierarchy. It was almost inevitable if you think about it. Some had inklings, or warnings from people in power in the teetering states, so they hired soldiers who'd already deserted their national armies. Equally foresightful, they made them civilians as quickly as they could, moving them into the ranks of middle-management before anyone got restless.

They were all afraid of religion though, that first wave of Firms, before the recent Consolidation. Maybe fear isn't the word, maybe it was just the kind of antipathy one power centre has for another. They were right to be worried, of course. But the Old Believers were tenacious. After the countries ended, churches, mosques, temples, they all remained as they were for a while. Then, of course, the Firms had to acquire them, turn them into production studios or flats. That didn't stop the Believers though. They still met, lived under bridges and on the fringes of cities, dug tunnels and lived in caves. The Firms ran a PR initiative aimed at stigmatising them - there's that analogy again, apologies. There were all kinds of names for them if you read the digi-archives: 'cucifuckboys', 'belief bros', 'submitters'. Well, they didn't submit so easily, it turned out, so the Firms did what they could to manage the problem, not without success stories. They certainly hired some of the right people.

*

I wouldn't say I work for the Firms, not now, though I did work for them. EuroCorp, for example, gave me an all-access clearance for the British Lighthouse, where they store all the manuscripts from Before. I don't know why they felt I was trustworthy, possibly because I charged them a lot of Coins. My job was to develop a meta theory of religious psychology so they could deal with the trouble that was gathering; Project Casaubon was the name of the operation. I had all the latest AIs at my disposal to try to formulate an easily translatable programme they could plug into their latest initiative, CryptoProphet1. It was hoped I could synthesise the ancient texts and develop a scripture they could 'discover' in a few decades time that would both invalidate previous scriptures - lots of 'contemporaneous' material would be referenced in my manuscript relating to the Old Works, discrediting them. The material would be 'discovered' at regular intervals and fed to the Idea Press to drive it home to everyone who wasn't paying close attention, or brooding about their lost salvations. The manuscript would also contain a handy set of principles that were just vague enough but just edifying enough to serve as the basis for a Firm-approved religion to diffuse the troubles. Again, the young would save us. When I spoke with the chair of the project, I brought this up.

'Madame Chair, do you not wonder why, if it is a generational matter, these problems keep recurring? We've had Darwin. We've had Einstein. We've had quantum mechanics. We've had nation-state official policies about atheism. Please don't misunderstand, I'm happy to do the work, but I don't want you to get the wrong idea about the ease of the project. You'll be spending a lot of Coins on it.'

'Sadiya, we appreciate your caution. We are confident that the material changes that we've brought about will create a major discontinuity with what has gone before. We feel that the failsafe of creating a replacement philosophy indemnifies us from the failures of past thinkers. We've done our homework'

'Homework. Yes, in doing that homework, I would ask, you're familiar with the French Revolution, I expect, no?'

'You expect well. Which aspect of it does your question concern?'

'It happened a little after the main event, it was called The Festival of the Supreme Being?'

'Oh yes. The entire Executive Council of this project had this fallacy specifically in mind when we designed our project.'

'Really? Just for clarification, I said "The Festival of the Supreme Being".'

'Absolutely. Examining the failures of design of the FoSB, we were able to determine that there were a number of flaws that doomed that project from the start. First, the reversal that Robespierre undertook: beginning a secular revolution only to install a makeshift deity when the going got, shall we say, rough? Secondly, the premise had no genuine content, how does one "celebrate" a 'Supreme Being"? It had all the downsides of the religion it sought to replace without any of the upsides. Terrible design. Absolutely shambolic. Thirdly, it was developer-led rather than crowdsourced. We fully intend to let our project go into the wild as early as feasible, and only to make minor iterative changes along its lifespan. We hope we have an open source and self-corrective architecture in place to implement whatever your research and writing produces. I could continue with my FoSB breakdown, but I do trust that this allays your worst fears?'

'Very much so. I'll get started on First Day.'

'We remain overjoyed.'

They paid me. Well. I did my research, but all the while, in the back of my mind, I knew there would be problems. I didn't know specifically what they would be; I just had a vague sense. And it was the knowledge of this vague sense that became the problem. To not know is to fill in spaces, and once one starts filling those spaces in, anything can happen. The project was launched ten years ago last month. It worked, sort of, but that was the problem. It had absolutely zero impact on the belief bros (and the submission sisters). If you order a delivery or order a MyCab,take a taxi, you're just as likely to see crosses and prayer beads as you were before - though it's only those professions where you do see them these days. Casaubon did become popular, especially with young people, but then they seemed to age out of it. You might say it became a 'rite of passage'.

Three years or so into the project being released into the wild the bugs crept in. Our fixes weren't being accepted by mainstreamers, people found flaws in the new texts, or actually chased the imaginary references (they always found them, of course, but they weren't always as well vetted as my original text, even good Hireds make mistakes). A few instances of that happening, and soon enough Casaubon became its own freelance project. Casaubon preachers, revivalists, fundamentalists, explicators all popped up. The Firms made use of them for a while, hiring the best ones and plugging them into people's streams, but there was always a new firebrand, an inspired visionary. The breakaway groups became bigger than the mainstream last year and some even joined with the Old Believers to resist Firm projects. Now they've started working with the Fighters. Some lead whole divisions. You see the big C that denoted Casaubonism on news blips and in Idea Press headlines. No one ever specifically fired me, but one day my project email stopped working. I didn't follow up with the board. I felt it was best to step back, to let nature, in its wisdom, take its course. It always does.

Ideators

The new regime was better. I understand it's about 11 micrograms now. Before, when they were still trying to get it right, it was kind of messy. Lots of crying. Some people just sat there, their eyes wide and unblinking and weren't normal for several days. Jerrik, the new CEO for idea production, has made the whole microdosing mandate a defining issue in his leadership, so he wasn't going to stop just because Darren from the style pages locked himself in a closet for an afternoon. That day, when Darren took his dose and almost immediately started sweating, tore off his shirt and ran into the eventuality closet, the doula told Jerrik what had happened and he came down from his office and addressed us.

"Folks, this is on me. We're trying new things, there are going to be bumps in the road, but I ask you to trust me. After all, trust is our business."

He kind of made a bow to us, or that's how I remember it at least, my own dose had me on a bit of a rollercoaster too. I don't think Jerrik was really wearing a flashing neon medallion when he spoke to us - he hasn't worn it since - but I can't be sure.

We heard Jerrik trying to coax Darren out of the closet while we all sat there, trying to manage our own states.

"Darren, it's Jerrik. Doing ok in there? You don't have to come out if you don't want to. It's ok. But if you'd like to tell me what's going on in there, I think maybe it might do you some good."

None of us could hear what Darren said, though Nadia from the Global desk said she could see inside his brain during the incident - if she's to be believed, he kept having visions of objects morphing into egg shapes while he tried desperately not to eat them. Eventually though, we heard Jerrik breaking the door down with the fire axe and dragging Darren to the Fun Ball Tub emptying it of balls and dousing him with water. He sat like that all afternoon. Jerrik assigned the intern to sit with him and to take down any ideas he had in the event he came up with something good while he was under.

Thankfully, Jerrik gave us a few days off to 'recalibrate' as he put it. The week after was when the new dose levels started. To show solidarity, Jerrik would always come in and dose with us in the room. The intern was always there too, so that no one missed anything and there was someone to hit the panic button if things got out of hand again. Things were much calmer though, even Darren, his face shining with perspiration like some kind of dolphin god, got through the new session with no trouble. As for me, I understood the principle, but it all seemed a little extreme.

Ideas, as Jerrik always reminded us, are power. The more ideas you have, the more power you have. Requiring the entire office to microdose three times a week was Jerrik's way of making sure we kept the power flowing. Idea Press companies are as competitive as any others. Don't let the CredCowboys in The City tell you otherwise. The microdose mandate was Jerrik's way of making sure we always had fresh ideas about - and for - the world, even if we didn't understand exactly what those ideas were all the time.

"Don't be afraid to think yourself into your thoughts," was one of the little mantras he had us memorise.

The Idea Press was booming now. There were market cycles, as with everything, but we were on an upswing and that was what had attracted Jerrik in the first place. Everyone knew his face from the Visionary Maestro courses he offered, or from the adverts that interrupted everyone's feeds promoting his new books or business ventures. I watched footage of him debating a Bright One once at some university once. I can't say he was a particularly sympathetic figure, but the sense of purpose and adventure that came across from the stage as he argued about the notion of a 'fact' with some professor of Firm History was more than a little infectious. He bought our company presumably with his pocket lint about a year ago during the downturn. He appeared on the office screens to tell us we were all about to go on an exciting adventure together, and that he'd saved our jobs.

"I acted because you produce the most valuable, and the most dangerous thing a society can produce, Ideas. I know there are people who use the term Idea Press ironically. I know it started as an insult, but you were right, everyone in this field, to embrace it and take it as a compliment. Yes: you make ideas. Yes, you manage ideas. Yes, you are ideas. And so are all of us. I can't wait to build the future with you!"

Jerrik greeted us all with a welcome gift. Everyone got a copy of a book by an old philosopher called Wittgenstein called The Philosophical Track or something like that. I never read it, I doubt many people in the office did, except maybe Alana, she likes to take work home with her. I leave the ideas at the office. When I'm home, give me HyperCricket, please. But I'll admit, I did read a few pages. Jerrik was big on telling us that the important thing to remember from Wittgenstein is that facts are made up of other facts. It's part of our jobs to find the facts inside the facts, to build ideas from those. Anyone can see the facts, but it takes a Visionary to see the facts beneath the facts. The thing that stuck with me about that book though was the last page. I flipped there right after I gave up on the first page. It ends on this line: 'Whereof one cannot speak, thereof one must be silent.' I had to wonder what Jerrik liked about that philosopher.

The first months were brutal. We went from a team of 40 to a team of 7. Only the most Idea-listic would survive, Jerrik told us. He changed all our titles from 'correspondent' or 'editor' to 'ideator'. Then we started having the Ideator of the Month ceremonies, then Ideator of the Day. At the moment it's Ideator of the Hour who gets a wage top up. There are rumours more cuts are around the corner and that it might go to an Ideator of the Quarter Hour soon.

The industry took notice though, and Jerrik won dozens of awards from Idea Press bodies and Firm Practice bodies. His speech for Sector Visionary of the Year at the end of 2077 was considered a classic of aspiration inspiration:

"You look at what I've done to a company and a sector in less than a year and you say that this is a monumental achievement. An epochal shift of direction. I look at it and I see the first step, the first baby step towards even greater change. Just wait. The ideas haven't even started."

Jerrik told the development department to go on the offensive, wherever we could make space for our stories, make them. He got in trouble for hacking people's mindstreams with our content, trying to use an experimental electromagnetic system to 'nudge' people's attention, but it blew over in about a week as all our competitors got into the game. It was intense, but it gave us a sense of purpose. A lot of our people won awards too, and we were the trend setters for the entire sector across all our coverage from business to culture to art. Jerrik told us that the emphasis had to be on production, not necessarily on content. Keep the ideas flowing and content would look after itself. 'It's umbrellas following rain, people. Simple laws of physics.' Oversupply was a feature not a bug. I remember him talking to me over my lunch blip after I'd had a slow week - 13 stories in four days. He brought it back to Wittgenstein: 'You remember what he said, no? "The world is everything that is the case. We're here to make that case, and make the world in the process. Step it up, Terry. Your world is shrinking.' I haven't written less than fifty stories a week since. They're not all classics ("From Contestant to Visionary: an afternoon in Hydrangea Maurin's life"), but Jerrik usually gives me a wink these days in the morning.

There seemed to be nothing we got wrong, until the Havering Crisis started. Every day was one story after another about the violence in Havering. Something about kids fighting over brand loyalties that escalated to the point where council order forces got involved. There were stories about drone strike victims, drone operators, embeds with professional brand militias, arguments about the use of health hitmen against council members. There seemed to be more stories than ever but no one ever really seemed to have a sense of what was going on. I tried to search out the origins of the conflict, but since Jerrik cancelled our office subscription to the Isle Information Archive, I had to rely on stories like the ones we write. It didn't help much.

The big issue of the moment was around general management. Bright Ones were in the streams constantly offering opinions about how to improve Firm positions so that things could be brought under control and the conflict could be kept from spreading ('Think Firms Can't Win Hearts and Minds? We Speak to a HypeBeast Round Table About The Havering Crisis'). The morning we moved into our new phase, we were all in the dosing room, about 90 minutes in. I'd just filed six different lists of best WretchTech tracks of all time, and Jerrik was almost boring into us with his eyes, 'We have to find a new take, one no one has had yet. THINK PEOPLE! THINK! IT'S THERE! WE JUST NEED TO FIND IT!!!!'

In the end, Alana had the idea. She was seated opposite Jerrik at the other end of the table, staring into the brilliant black surface of the painting Jerrik had bought for the dosing room for inspiration, "What if we support the councils?"

No one said anything. I looked over at Jerrik's face. It seemed to pass through dozens of expressions in microseconds. It was a brutal idea. Almost primeval in its simplicity. Of course, the Bright Ones and those types at the universities would hate it, but anyone with a grain of honesty in their soul knew that was part of the point, part of why we existed, to play the endless game of May I? with the respectables. Besides, Jerrik would be more than happy to offer them a right of reply on our feed for an entirely reasonable fee. But even as he began to settle into a decisive smile, and even as he pointed his finger-guns at Alana and said, "Direct hit! Get on it!" something was troubling him beneath the surface, a rumbling that might be trivial or might be the opening of a rift in the earth's surface. To let them in again, the old ideas, governance, even nations, with all the profane logics they contained, there were risks even a confirmed visionary like Jerrik couldn't entirely foresee. But his smile broadened, and it deepened as it set. He seemed almost in awe now, of this catalytic idea. These were the whole reason any of us were in this business at all. And besides, even if things got hot, someone - no doubt someone around this very table - would come up with an even more powerful idea that would stop the worst from happening. That was the one thing he was sure of.

The Next

William appeared at just the right moment. This was among his best qualities. Gabriel was sitting in the living room, looking out over the bowls and decanters arranged on the quartz table. He found himself scrutinising the trees, the way the shadows fell, the sun as it slumped across the trunks and threaded among the branches and the leaves. William walked in from the kitchen. Everything seemed in order. Perfect order. It was such a relief.

"Is it right," Gabriel asked.

William walked over and brought his head level with Gabriel's and looked out into the trees.

'Right, sir?'

'The light.'

'Is the light right?'

'Not the light itself, no. The presence of the light. The angles are all accurate, look. Accurate, but are they right?'

He showed William his phone screen where the source image of the trees was displayed, Gabriel slid his finger over the image and brought one picture of the trees and the forest away from the other.

'They fit perfectly. When you lay one over the other, they're identical, but when you bring it up to three dimensions, and you project it out, something's wrong. Something's just not…right.'

William looked at the pictures again. Gabriel handed him his phone and William dried his hands on his apron and did the same trick as Gabriel, pulling one forest off the other. He couldn't tell them apart, which was the source and which was the model? They seemed a perfect match, certainly, but when he looked up at the trees reflecting on the sliding door to the patio, he could see what Gabriel meant.

'Perhaps it's the glass, sir?'

'The glass. It could be the glass. Let's see.'

Gabriel stood up and William understood that it was his job to follow Gabriel out onto the patio to see the trees up close, 'in the real', so to speak.

Gabriel opened the shutter and they stood on the concrete beneath the thick stone dome above.

Gabriel narrowed his eyes. He rubbed his fingers on his chin. He was a parody of a man carefully considering something. He looked wordlessly over to his Domestic Executive.

'Is it right?'

William looked into the trees. He squinted. Perhaps 'right' was the wrong word...

'Is it the Forest of Dean or not?'

'I...I've never been, sir.'

'No. No, I suppose you haven't, not in that way at least,' Gabriel lightly put his hand on William's shoulder as if to console him for the things he'd missed out on. Twenty years Gabriel's junior, he'd only known the conflict. He was born below ground.

The DomEx tried to sound upbeat.

'I don't know whether the others will know the Forest either, sir. At any level of detail.'

'Won't know it? Of course they won't know it. It's not about whether they know it. It's about the light. The forest is incidental. I'm an engineer not a...what...'

'An ecologist, sir?'

'I'm not an ecologist. No. Thank you. But, I must say you can be terribly obtuse sometimes. Do you not see that it's a matter of fidelity? A matter of design. A matter of Art.'

'You've adjusted the brightness?'

'Yes.'

'A gradient?'

'Of course!'

'One hesitates to be obtuse, sir, but it is entirely possible that you've come as close to what you're seeking as is physically possible. There are certain limits that technology can only —'

'Limits? Certain limits the technology can only "approach", was that your next word?'

'Something in that direction, sir.'

'I'm an Innovator, William. Everyone who will be here tonight, they're all Innovators. Innovators look at the world through different eyes. We don't settle. We don't accept there are "limits" to what is possible. We wouldn't be where we are today if Innovators settled. We are different. Is that something you can understand?'

William was silent. He looked at the trees, and the light. Gabriel squatted down and looked up at the trees. William could see he was still out of countenance. Indeed, there was something off about the trees. Perhaps more than one thing.

"I should see to the kitchen, sir."

"Yes. You should."

William disappeared. Gabriel looked down at his hands, they seemed guilty to him. He put them in the pockets of his dinner jacket. He looked out into the Forest of Dean again. It was perfect. Perhaps it was too perfect? Perhaps that was the problem. It was a problem he'd had over the years. He'd created so much to enrich humankind. He'd designed the first fully functional no-crew containership. He pioneered the cog-pay system almost all businesses now used, now that no one trusted hard currency anymore. He'd even played a major role in designing the nano-satellite system that allowed space speccing for the first time. He was the first trillionaire born in the Isles and he was proud of that. He should be. He'd done a lot, but the one thing he hadn't done was 'settle' and he wouldn't settle tonight. He would get the light right.

After an hour of minor adjustments and toggling, Gabriel grudgingly reverted to the filter settings he'd had at first. Perhaps it had been right all along. Sometimes he got things right on the first try and it took someone else to show him. It was the fate of the perfectionist. To be right but to think you're wrong. But it nagged, that strange, overly cheery light, there was something…unnatural about it. Perhaps they wouldn't notice (they would). Perhaps it was enough that he'd produced a simulation that was correct in every detail but volumetrics (it wasn't). After a few drinks, no one would notice (they would). He'd keep them inside for a bit, for drinks and some music. After a glass or two, he could even possibly draw their attention to it, even suggest they go outside. He could blame the glass for the distortion, or if they were drinking they'd chalk it all up to their own perceptions (surely). By the time they came out to smoke, vape, or to get some of the fresh air he had generated with his filtering system, no one wouldn't know the difference. Besides, they only had their own memories to go on, what it looked like above. It would be alright. He just had to handle it carefully, with an engineer's eye.

*

In the kitchen William was still seeing to the food. It would be seven courses with a variety of canapés. Sourcing had gotten quite difficult since the trouble above, but Gabriel had hired a light consultant months ago (could he call him up now, for his opinion on the forest?); functionally, the allotments he administered - this was his job, not William's - were operating at a capacity that allowed him to actually sell off his excess produce and derivatives for a profit. When he was younger he'd read about Innovators who had begun in farming, but perhaps this was the new way. Then, you began with the soil, and your ideas created a distance between you and it. Now, it was the inverse. Brilliance in business led you back to the earth and its unbending material truths. The symmetry made him smile for a moment, before he allowed himself to consider the troubles above, the whole reason he and the other crucial Innovators had needed to build this Below World. The incidents in London twenty years ago had been the trigger. Drone strikes in Havering, leading to unrest throughout the Isle Firm Zone. Malcontents around the world coming from the outlands into the cities to turn back various clocks into the confusion that preceded the global Time Zone.

No one, not him, not any of the Bright Ones he went to uni with or worked with, had understood how fragile the webs of exchange Firm governance had created were. As things got worse, academics had spent precious time orating on the endless resilience of the new Firm politicraft form, but Gabriel and some of the other Innovators noticed the fraying in time. They produced the technologies that prolonged The Stability for decades, but then, as more and more outlanders came in and brought their violence with them, their bottomless irrationality, the time came, and those who could escape did. There weren't many, and building the Below World was a feat of engineering that involved a kind of collectivism that cut against everything Gabriel and the others had learned in their professional lives. Still, survival focuses the mind, especially brilliant ones. But survival was for Simples and Contestants. Beauty was what Gabriel always prided his designs on. He didn't want merely to make things people could use, but things people loved. Things people would want. Desire is the mother of beauty after all.

Gabriel had been proud of the ways his models had contributed to the achievements of Below World light engineering, how he'd found a way to tap the fault lines beneath the Pacific to work as a kind of permanent generator. He'd created a light production system that could be operated at scale with minimal energy waste; beautiful, necessary, efficient. It was one thing to be an engineer, almost all the surviving Innovators were, Gabriel still saw his work as a kind of art. Beauty is a home that lives inside you, a place that can shelter you and give solace through even the most unimaginable calamities, the kind the world was living through now. Gabriel felt that his work could play a role in creating that home for everyone forced into the Below World, those who had created so much, and who expected so much. That was why the light on the trees had been so important. Light is a fundamental property of the universe. Light and time are nearly the same thing. To not see the light from the sun for fifteen years - that was almost how long it was now - the human body could be said to lose its mind. Gabriel wanted to give the sense of true, organic illumination back to his friends, back to whatever of humanity that was surviving now in the Below World. An evening in the sun, it was something everyone deserved, but only those who had no appreciation of it could claim today.

Gabriel walked into the kitchen. William's head was in the oven. He was checking on the butternut squash and halloumi-sage tarts.

'William, I wanted to say, I'm sorry about earlier. I was...well, It's just, sometimes, well, you know, sometimes...'

'Yes, sir. The burden of vision may only appear to be light from outside.'

'Well put. I must tell you sometime about the difficulty we had in producing the first shuttle race. I was in a partnership with Old Pete Seeley at the time.'

'The clock is ticking, sir.'

'Oh, yes! Of course. I'll leave you to it, William. I know you have a busy night. I'll just, I should have a drink and put on some music.'

'Of course, sir.'

'Any requests?'

'Requests, sir?'

'Music you'd like to hear?'

'Your judgment is best.'

Gabriel opened a fresh bottle of gin and walked back into the living room. He heard the bell go.

'Don't trouble yourself, William! I'll get it,' he called, departing for the long hallway before William called his own muffled answer back, but whatever he said was lost in the echoes of the concrete corridor.

*

'Sorry we're early,' said Eric Joven, passing a bottle of ancient Lafite to Gabriel who took his hand and helped him and his companion up the security step into the foyer.

'Are you early?'

'He makes a point of being early so he can draw attention to it by apologising,' said his companion, who Gabriel hadn't met before.

They walked down the hallway into the living room. Gabriel felt self conscious for the first time about the length of his entry corridor. Longer was in vogue a few years ago when the works on his place started, but now people were opting for shorter entries with a security cocktail of blast doors and non-lethal gasses in the event of breaches. Gabriel only had the one door and the security step. The step was a stupid idea. He let the salesman talk him into it, 'cost effective solution to intrusions, buys a full minute with a laser trip. And I don't have to tell you, time is money.' Reflecting, Gabriel now saw this as a veiled insult instead of a sales truism.

"This is really cozy," Eric said.

Gabriel and Eric met nearly twenty five years ago at the Global Firm Gathering in St. Gallen. Eric was giving a talk about the distributed awareness system he was creating at the time. Of course it was a massive success, all the Firms wanted in, some needed it for environmental reasons, some for efficiency issues, some for what they would cryptically refer to as 'exogenous emergences'. Eric was good with a crowd, he could get people to believe in things, especially the improbable.

Gabriel offered him a gin and Eric almost snatched it out of his hand.

'Easy,' his companion said, 'Eric's microdosing.'

'Oh?'

'It's work-related, Gabe, it just helps me ideate.'

'Eric is planning a new telecoms system for the tunnels.'

'It's nothing really, just a way to overcome some of the troubles the blast walls create. Hoping we can exploit photons. It's early days. Very early days.'

'Was it a good ideation though?'

'Very. Breakthroughs of all kinds. You don't dose, do you Gabe?'

'It takes me out of myself.'

'And what's wrong with that? Nothing like a little "not-me" time.'

Eric's companion was laughing, 'I'm Val by the way.'

'She's the one who got me dosing again, after all these years.'

'How did you meet…down here?'

'Tunnel of Love.'

'Of course.'

'We bought the stock. Everyone down here is on it. Aren't you Gabe?'

'I…I've been busy.'

'You should. It's got to be lonely out here, just you and your man, what's his name?'

'William.'

'I'm sure he's on it.'

'Possibly,' it wasn't something Gabriel had ever given any thought to, somehow the thought disturbed him, he didn't know why.

'You should at least buy stock ever since J'Nese Winters got an exchange going down here, it's been nonstop.'

'J'Nese is coming tonight. He should be at least.'

'You two will have a lot to talk about,' Eric said to Val, 'Val's been doing very well with commodities lately.'

'Commodities?'

'Absolutely,' Val said, 'the market is bigger than it's been since we came down here. We think we could officially start offering securities, but J'Nese, or his team, they'd have to approve. Listings and all of that. Licenses.'

The doorbell rang again. This time William appeared from the kitchen, but Gabriel told him not to worry. Eric took the occasion to request another round of drinks and William disappeared back into the kitchen. A market in commodities securities in the tunnels? The thought set Gabriel on edge. The idea of large scale agriculture underground was bad enough, but the way it sounded, Val was counting on some kind of underground population explosion, unless she was selling to the surface, which made no sense. Which was the more troubling thought, that life above was being exactly reproduced down here, or that his friends believed it could be?

It was Hayashi Mori and his companion at the door. They brought Gabriel a bottle of whisky and some night orchids from their hothouse. Hayashi was very excited to chat to Eric. He'd read a piece by him in the Idea Press about the prospect of the singularity coming in the next year, "It was the first time in fifteen years I've felt real hope,' he said. Gabriel waved to Eric and Hayashi and his friend started down toward them, their shoes making an eerie rattle in the corridor as they shrank. Gabriel was about to close the door when he heard Grace Powers' voice echoing down the tunnel "I think it's here." Gabriel called out to her and she went quiet suddenly, knowing she was being heard.

'Gabriel, at last,' she said when she appeared out of the eerie orange light that illuminated the tunnels.

'You weren't lost were you?'

'Lost? How do you get lost in a tunnel?'

'You'd find a way,' her companion said. She was a short-haired woman - no, Gabriel definitely hadn't met her. Sometimes, underground, time melted into itself, and so did faces.

Grace squeezed his arm gently and smiled and inspected the room down the corridor. She introduced her friend as Maggie and they all made their way down the long entrance hall..

Standing in the centre of the room, next to the quartz table William was offering a tray of drinks to everyone.

'Gabe, we were just picking the brain of your man here.'

'Eric asked him if he'd quit working for you if he found out we could all go above ground again.'

Everyone was tittering. Gabriel looked over Eric's shoulder toward the patio, without looking him in the eye, he said, 'And what did he say?'

Eric nodded toward William.

'Well, I simply said that I'd never been above. I said that I expected it would be quite strange. For some of us, I suppose down looks rather like up does to you.'

Gabriel smiled, unsure why he was smiling. He wasn't sure if it was funny, just that it was enough to make his friends laugh.

'You'll find out soon enough, fella. I expect major developments soon. Very soon,' Eric said, winking at Val.

Gabriel realised again there was no music on and gestured to turn on the sound system. It hummed to life and Hayashi seized immediate control of the playlist. Within a few minutes, Egon Crane from EndOverEnd Investments, and J'Nese from the exchange arrived with a gaggle of people in tow. Almost everyone was there, but where was Lex Lawler? Of course he would be late, but would he also be totally battered on some new psychedelic he was synthesising in his bathroom. Gabriel remembered a horrific New Year he'd spent at Lex's bunkalow when he'd spiked everyone's drink with the lysergic ginseng he'd developed. Perhaps Eric was looking forward to it, but it held no appeal for Gabriel. Gabriel had vomited, several times, that fateful New Year, much to Lex's amusement. A day of pictures flowed into his inbox from people at the party, each with a different angle on his despair. The worst was the overwhelmingly horrible sensation he'd had of 'remembering the future'. He had told no one about it, but he had a strange flashback to that moment now, as he waited for Lex to arrive and Hayashi's music played and everyone drank and pitched new projects to each other. It was like it had been before, only now in an uncanny, ersatz way. Perhaps it was just him. The nerves of playing host setting him on edge.

The door went again and it was Lex. He smiled and hugged Gabriel. Gabriel felt something squish when Lex pressed against him.

'Oh no. Oh NO! I'd printed some swordfish for you, but," he looked into the bag, "I didn't wrap it properly.'

'You had it…in your pocket?'

'Blazer pocket. Yes. So it would appear.'

'Well, William can sort you out with a new coat. We'll get this one in the wash.'

'It would have been so good,' Lex said, looking at the fish pool gathering at his feet. His trousers were now part of the incident as well.

'It's the thought that counts.'

'Which thought?'

Gabriel led him into the living room and everyone cheered when they saw him. Lex's 3-D printed food project was central to Hayashi's plan to establish a moon base once the singularity came, so they started in immediately. In Hayashi's projections, it was less than a decade away. So he was particularly glad to see Lex and gave him a big bear hug, causing more swordfish leakage. 'Proof of concept,' he said to general laughter. William bobbed in with more drinks and, at Gabriel's prompting, swabbed up the fish juice. Lex winked at him. William simply nodded and disappeared with Lex's blazer.

Gabriel's friends were all in high spirits as a nicely eerie WraithWave track played. It was, he thought, an ideal warm up for the evening's surprise musical guest. Gabriel had hired the producer Ghostswag to generate an ambient soundscape for the Below World's rapper poet of the moment, Calvin O. Italy. Italy was composed of the back catalogues of ancient legends of hip hop like Rakim, Tupac, MC Search, and Common and the artist's aesthetic was an amalgam of styles Ghostswag had fused according to trend forecasts he'd developed in collaboration with speccing firms. WretchCore was the name of the aesthetic, a more introspective, cerebral take on GroundGlass. At 21.00 Ghostswag would upload Italy to Gabriel's entertainment system and he would achieve his first recorded embodiment. Gabriel was quietly very excited to be a part of it. He'd studied rap as part of his Uni electives, and he always found the interplay of structure and flow fascinating from a technical perspective, but as he got older, he became more engaged with the actual lyrics. The words, he'd thought initially, had been means to an end but now he understood they often had a coherent meaning, if one chose to look - though admittedly why would one with so many new art forms emerging, and there were infinite mindstreams you could tune into even in the Below.

At exactly 21.00 Gabriel's lights went down. Ghostswag was in charge of the system now. Gabriel heard the sound of birds - actual birds, it all seemed so long ago now, but he remembered when birds existed. How could he have forgotten? But he had. There they were again, now. Gabriel caught himself holding tears back. First it was birds, then it was the ominous, shadowy synth that defined WretchCore and its parent genre GroundGlass. Then came the thundering collision of metals that formed the spine of the beats. Gabriel was almost overwhelmed with the sound, he was transfixed on the empty space where Italy would soon appear. Seconds later, the lights came up and before them stood Calvin O. Italy. Italy looked them over as they sat perched on Gabriel's sofa, cross-legged on the floor, gathered in huddles by the glass door to the patio, Innovators in the gaze of an innovation. Italy's look was almost haughty but still open. His flashing polychrome eyes scanned each of their faces, almost as if Italy planned to speak to them personally and individually. When he came to Gabriel, he cocked his head back in a kind of approving acknowledgement. It was a moment before Gabriel realised Italy's head was a dolphin's head. A princess dolphin. He remembered, as a boy, learning about their extinction. A moment later it was a white rhino's head looking out at them from the mix of survival gear and streetwear Ghostswag had dressed Italy in. Italy morphed again before saying anything, he was a bald eagle, then he was a snow leopard. When the rap started, Italy was a blue whale. They'd all gone extinct decades ago but now they were here, almost living, but more than living. Italy opened their mouths and produced a thin, mournful note, a keening whale dirge, and then came the lyrics. The narrative of the song focussed on the hunting and killing of endangered species. Every time a new species would be named, Italy's face would change and become that of the hunted animal. The story unfolded like a tale of gangland murders with humans in the role of a crazed gang, drunk on the shuddering joy of violence for its own sake. Italy would unfold the narrative and then the chorus would come over the metallic skeletal beat:

Cause and Effects
Everything out here connects
Names is down on the list, put the target in the text
Yeah, you come for me today,
Check your aim and best not miss,
Or find yourself miss a trick,
Find your self in a fix,
Predator today,
now you the one who better pray
Better get you your way,
if not, can only say
It come right back right away
It's just cause and effect,
All serve and no protect,
Its just cause and effects
Come for me, get you wrecked
only one thing to expect
Cause and effect

Y'all Next (y'all next)!

The final line: *Y'all next.* Repeated over and over again in the speakers after Italy disappeared. Then the lights came up. No one could move. Lex Lawler was weeping. Only William appearing from the kitchen to collect drinks and bring another round brought everyone back to their present reality. Gabriel felt that now was the moment. At last!

'Everyone! I...I want to show you something,' he said, 'Please, come outside,' he said, before realising how ridiculous, how desperate that must sound.

People obeyed and formed a small queue by the sliding door. Gabriel activated the projection and the trees appeared. The silence continued. Gabriel led everyone out into the forest. They stepped into the projection. The trees seemed to recede as they stepped closer to them.

'It's...it's so beautiful,' said Terence.

'You could almost touch them,' said J'Nese stepping forward toward the low, bowing summery limbs, 'But you can't, can you?'

Gabriel shook his head. He felt the tightness of the skin of his face from his smile, 'I haven't got the depth quite right,' Gabriel heard himself volunteering. It was like a confession, but the moment felt right for confessions.

Grace and her companion walked out into the trees, she was just visible through the fissures of light that cut through the trunks of pines, she looked back toward the living room and put her hand flat against her brow, 'It's like it's moving away from us.'

'There are a lot of bugs,' Gabriel said.

'No ticks, I hope,' said Lex who was more like himself now.

Gabriel paid him no attention. He looked out on all his friends, all the Innovators moving through the trees, his trees. No, not his trees. The trees, the trees of the Forest of Dean. It wasn't real, but they seemed to take the collective decision that it was real enough. They wandered around in the projection, oblivious to their own shadows slicing through the scenery.

William found Gabriel on the patio.

'I think dinner is ready, sir.'

'They love it, William. They're absolutely enthralled.'

'Well, sir, I would expect nothing less.'

Gabriel patted William on the shoulder and nodded toward the kitchen. He called to the Innovators to come out of the woods for dinner. Everyone found places at the long steel table and sat down. William brought out the courses and conversations meandered along in a strangely soporific way, as if everyone had been at Eric's mushroom stash. Minutes before they'd weeping at Calvin O. Italy, then making their way through Gabriel's forest. Now they were themselves again. There was nothing wrong with it, nothing at all, it was a dinner party after all, but Gabriel found he couldn't relax. He'd start chatting to someone and then get distracted, first by the memory of Italy's song, not the lyrics so much as the birds that had come before it. How they'd tricked him for a moment, and it was a trick, and how he'd believed it. How he'd been fooled by a kind of hope. How hope had seemed to quickly curdle into something else, in the song and beyond the song. It struck him that however perfect the trees were, the silence was a problem, a disturbance of its own. He'd have to bring in a sound designer so that the acoustics could be improved. A forest without birdsong, the idea was filling him with horror. He waved to William to put on some music. He needed something to clear his head, some kind of sound now. The voices of his friends, laughing, philosophising, all seemed horrible to him now as they ricocheted off the hidden walls and domes of the room. The room seemed to be asserting its presence more aggressively, as if it were trying to remind him that it was still there, nothing he could do could hide it or make it go away. The bunker was everywhere. He could create a place, it seemed to be saying, but only in a space. And them, their heads all filled with dreams of it all ending soon, of going back above ground, the wars being over, the dullards fighting dead or put back into their place in the outlands. They'd come back up, above ground, he and his friends, and they'd be richer than before, much richer indeed than before they'd gone below. They could do anything, everything, even. But what would it be when he first stepped into whatever the Forest of Dean was now, even if it was perfectly preserved, even if the wars above hadn't touched it. What would it be like when he stepped in among the trees and heard that silence again. The birds were still gone. Even in the most optimistic dreams of cloning, reconstitution, they were decades away. The silence would be there perhaps for the rest of his life. He could hear it now, looking out on his own Forest. It was deafening. Somehow, Grace was staring at him now, as though he were mad. Had he been saying all this out loud?

'Darling, you don't need to blush, but do at least congratulate me.'

'Congratulate you?'

'Isn't that the done thing when one has a baby?'

'Of course! Of course. Yes, I'll—' Gabriel stood up and tapped his wine glass with his knife. "Everyone," he said in a voice that sounded ridiculously stentorian as he began. He looked at Grace as if for some kind of rescue. She just inched her shoulders up and shook her head as if to say, 'you've started, you may as well finish.'

'Grace is….Grace, she's…she's'

'I'm bloody pregnant, now go back to drinking!'

Everyone cheered. Lex clumsily attempted to play 'Happy Birthday' on the unevenly filled glasses which earned him a grimace from Hayashi. William quickly collected them and brought in a fresh, refilled set. A child, Gabriel thought, it was a beautiful thought if you allowed yourself to think about it, a commitment to the idea that not all was lost. But the wars wouldn't end, not the way Eric thought they would, anyway - he was loudly extemporising a post-war scenario to half the table. If the wars ended they would end because some greater calamity stopped them, not the singularity, not careful planning, not effective product distribution, not optimism and optimisation. They would end because the death they thrived on would triumph. They would end when there was nothing more to fight over. They would end, most probably, in silence. Gabriel felt ashamed of the darkness that kept climbing back into his mind. There was beauty all around him, even in this truncated world they'd created. He could see that, but it somehow made everything worse. The party went on for sometime longer, but then J'Nese made his excuses. He had to open the markets up tomorrow bright and early. This was taken as a kind of cue; soon everyone was leaving. Gabriel stood up to wish them well on their trip through the tunnels. Hayashi assured him he'd get Lex home in one piece. Grace took his hand when she left and said, 'I can't wait to take the baby for a walk in your forest.' Gabriel smiled and told her he'd be sure to have a fully interactive beta version ready by the time her child was born, he promised. Everyone was gone now. Gabriel was alone with William. William asked if there was anything more Gabriel needed from him.

'I don't think so. No, not really,' then, 'William, just quickly, when Eric was joking with you earlier, what you said, that 'up looked like down' to you, what exactly did you mean by it?'

'Sir, it just came to me. Rather spur of the moment. But thinking of it, I suppose I was trying to express the sense that those of us who have never been up above, I think we've learned a bit from you. From your generation, if I may, sir. Perhaps we've learned not to believe the grass is always greener in quite the way some of your friends seem to.'

Gabriel smiled at his man. He gathered a few glasses and William took this as the signal to get the tray for him and start clearing up. As he put the glasses down ,Gabriel said, 'I see, William, the grass may not be greener. Indeed, there may not be grass at all.'

'Indeed, sir,' William said, and he disappeared again into the kitchen.

Gabriel settled into the bilious cushions of his sofa. He scrolled his screen to see if there were any messages for the tomorrow that was sure to come. Ghostswag had been in touch. He wanted to know how Gabriel liked Italy's performance. Gabriel told him it had moved him greatly. Ghostswag sent a riot of ecstatic emojis. 'Here's the full album,' he wrote. Gabriel put on the music right away, letting the playlist begin as it was supposed to, but then he hunted out 'Y'all Next'. He listened with tears in his eyes as the birdsong began, accompanied by the comforting clatter of William at the dishes in the kitchen. Gabriel thought about Grace's child wandering through his Forest someday, growing up in this underworld, learning how to live by means of the teachings of aliens. He looked out at the darkened landing where the forest had been, there was nothing to see but his own reflection in the sliding glass door. He turned on the forest again, and looped the first few seconds of 'Y'all Next' . He let the music seep out into the darkness beyond and disperse into his silent trees.

Acknowledgements from the Author

Thank you to everyone at Arcadia Missa, particularly to Ruth Pilston for her editing work. Thanks also to Nicholas Midgley, Elvia Wilk, Jack Clarke, Vijay Khurana, Emily Waddell, Daisy Sainsbury, Madeleine Watts, Tom Vandeputte, Flavia Dzodan, and Eva Hoonhout.

AM
PUBLISHING

* 9 7 8 1 8 3 8 2 8 4 0 1 5 *

BV - #0134 - 231025 - C0 - 203/127/7 - PB - 9781838284015 - Matt Lamination